Southern
Indian
Myths
and
Legends

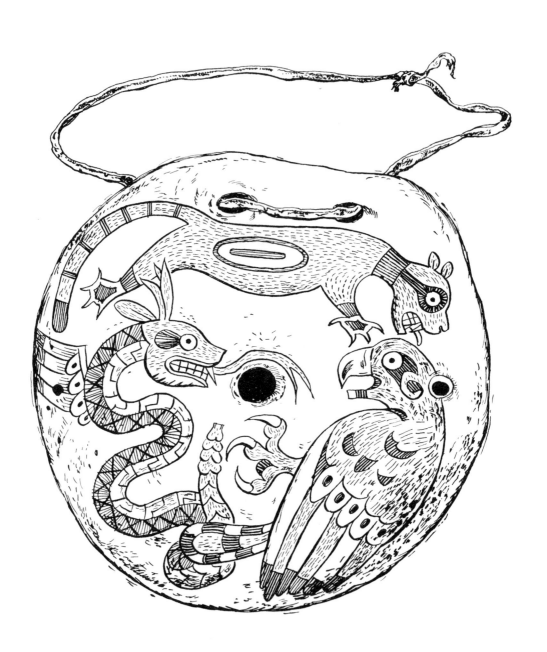

Southern Indian Myths and Legends

Compiled and edited by
Virginia Pounds Brown
and
Laurella Owens

Illustrated by **Nathan H. Glick**

NewSouth Books

Montgomery

NewSouth Books
105 S. Court Street
Montgomery, AL 36104

ISBN 978-1-58838-253-5

Publishing history: This book was originally published in 1985 by
Beechwood Books, Leeds, Alabama, with the ISBN 0-912221-
02-X. The current edition closely follows the original design by
Bob and Faith Nance but was retypeset and the pages recomposed
digitally for modern printing methods.

Library of Congress Control Number: 2014934461

Library of Congress Cataloging in Publication Data (for
Beechwood Books edition)
Main entry under title:
Southern Indian myths and legends.
    Bibliography: p.
    Includes index.
    Summary: Presents fifty-nine stories from Choctaw,
Chickasaw, Cherokee, Creek, and Seminole mythology, in such
categories as creation and migration of tribes, the origin of
tobacco, fire, and other gifts of the Great Spirit, and monsters and
heroes.
    1. Indians of North America—Southern States—Legends.
[2. Indians of North America—Southern States—Religion and
mythology] I. Brown, Virginia Pounds. II. Owens, Laurella.
III. Glick, Nathan H., ill.

Printed in the United States of America
by Versa Press

Contents

For our mothers,
Doreen Hosford Owens and Virginia Lawson Pounds
And to the memory of Elloie Jeter Bradshaw,
beloved by the Poarch Band of Creek Indians
East of the Mississippi

Preface

While researching our previous book *The World of the Southern Indians*, we became aware of the great amount of material on southern Indian myths and legends buried in government publications and scholarly journals. We discovered also that no collection bringing together stories from the main southern tribes had been attempted. In fact, very few stories from southern Indians have been included in any North American Indian myth collection.

Because the original culture of the southern Indians has been greatly changed by white contact, we realized our main sources for the ancient stories must be in written, not oral, information. We have searched mainly in Bureau of American Ethnology publications, folklore journals, and manuscripts in the Alabama Archives and History Department. Of these sources the most valuable were the Bureau of American Ethnology materials. Field workers from the Bureau in the late nineteenth and early twentieth centuries compiled extensive collections of southern Indian folklore. At that time Indian storytellers were available to them, people who still remembered tribal stories, though usually in bits and pieces.

We have tried to bring together stories from as many tribes as possible. Of the 59 tales included here, 18 are Cherokee, 21 Creek (and allied tribes), nine Choctaw, six Seminole, six Chickasaw, one Catawba, one Chitimacha.

The Cherokee stories required little editing. Their compiler, James A. Mooney, had already woven the different versions he had heard (sometimes as many as 7) into complete stories. On the other hand, stories of the Creeks, Chickasaws, and Choctaws were, for the most part, fragmented and disjointed, requiring reconstruction and retelling. Their compiler, John R. Swanton, unlike Mooney, recorded many versions of a story without attempting to unify them.

In putting together this collection, we have seen our job as one of evaluating, selecting, editing, rewriting, and providing help to readers in the form of notes and introductions. As we did in *The World of the Southern Indians*, we have tried to bring together scattered material and present it in interesting and readable form. It is our hope that this book will bring about a much needed recognition of southern Indian tales.

For assistance in preparation of this book we are indebted to the following: Margaret Miller; Mary Bess Paluzzi and Yvonne Crumpler, Southern Collection, Birmingham Public Library; Mary Lou Miller and Virginia Jackson, Mervyn H. Sterne Library, University of Alabama in Birmingham; Elizabeth Wells and Shirley Hutchens, Harwell G. Davis Library, Samford University; Edwin C. Bridges, director, Alabama Department of Archives and History. We are especially grateful to Azilee M. Weathers, Government Documents librarian at Samford University, for her help.

We are particularly indebted to J. Anthony Paredes, professor and chairman, Department of Anthropology, the Florida State University, Tallahassee, for his reading of the manuscript and his suggestions.

Myth-Keeping
Introduction

More Indians have lived in what is now the southern USA than any other area north of Mexico. Yet we know little about southern Indians. After the removal of the five great tribes (Chickasaws, Choctaws, Creeks, Cherokees, Seminoles) to the west, white people seemed to want to forget these people forced from their tribal lands.

After the 1840s, only isolated pockets of Indians remained in the South. These small groups kept to themselves, which suited the non-Indian community, who did not welcome reminders of a departed people.

But today we see the Indians differently. We want to know about southern Indian history and culture.

Much of what we want to know about southern Indians we can learn from their myths and legends. Having no written language, tribes depended on word-of-mouth communication to keep alive their traditions—their history, their beliefs, their ceremonies and rituals. More than any other source, their stories tell us how Indians perceived themselves and what they thought about the world around them.

Myths (as distinct from legends) are the oldest stories of a tribe, reaching back to an earlier world. They have their roots in a tribe's ancient religious rites and beliefs. Myths of the southern Indians answer such questions as how the earth was formed, how life began, how corn came. All world mythologies have sprung up answering such questions.

The sacred myths of the southern Indians could be told only

by medicine men or myth-keepers such as Swimmer of the Cherokees. The Cherokee story of the origin of corn and hunting was so sacred that those who heard it were required to purify themselves.

As tribes grew older, legends were added to myths. Some legends were tales of the exploits of a hero, either a man or a beast possessing supernatural powers. The role of hero among the southern Indians frequently fell to Rabbit, whose tricks delighted storytellers and listeners. Other legends have some basis in historical fact, as the migration legends. Some may be tied to definite geographical locations, such as some of the monster stories of the Cherokees. Legends grow and change. It is important to remember that even today stories are being told by small groups of Indians in the South about their tribal heritage. These may be tomorrow's legends.

Myths and legends reveal the close kinship among the southern Indian tribes. All told similar stories. They are told, however, with distinctive tribal differences.

The most valuable sources of southern Indian myths and legends are the works of John R. Swanton and James A. Mooney. An anthropologist with the Bureau of American Ethnology, Swanton collected many Creek stories between 1908 and 1914 from Creeks living in Oklahoma, Texas, and Louisiana. Swanton also depended heavily on the work of William O. Tuggle, who collected Creek stories from 1879–83. Tuggle served as a lawyer to the Creeks. In addition to Creek collections, Swanton published books on the Choctaws and Chickasaws, which contain myths and legends. He performed a monumental task in bringing together thousands of Indian stories.

James A. Mooney, an ethnologist, also with the Bureau of American Ethnology, collected Cherokee stories on the Cherokee reservations in North Carolina between 1887 and 1890, and in the Indian Territory (Oklahoma). Among his informants were four remarkable storytellers, three of whom had heard the tales as boys tending the fires of the myth-keepers and priests.

Another valuable source for stories is the work of the scholar-missionary Henry Sale Halbert, who lived as a teacher among the Choctaws in Mississippi in the late 1800s. Halbert tirelessly collected Choctaw customs and folklore at a time when only a few Indians remembered the old days. Halbert worked at the Alabama Archives and History Department from 1904-18, where he continued his writing about the Choctaws.

H. B. Cushman was another missionary who spent much of his life among the Choctaws. He was, in Swanton's words, "our only authority on certain phases of ancient Choctaw life."

The world we see reflected in the myths and legends of the South's first people is a fascinating world, populated with monsters, spirits, talking animals. These tales, reaching deep into the heart and soul of a people, give us insights into human history and destiny.

Unless otherwise noted, the sources for Creek, Chickasaw, and Choctaw stories are from the works of John R. Swanton. The source for Cherokee stories is James A. Mooney's Myths of the Cherokee. *See Story Sources in Bibliography.*

The Southern Tribes

The Cherokees lived in the mountains of west North Carolina, east Tennessee, northeast Alabama, and north Georgia. More successfully than any other southern tribe they adapted their way of life to accommodate the whites. They expected to be allowed to stay on their land in spite of the Removal Act of 1830, but in 1838 thirteen thousand Cherokees went west. About 5,000 Cherokees live today on the Qualla Reservation in North Carolina, descendants of the Cherokees who hid in the mountains from the US Army in 1838.

The Chickasaws were a small tribe, but they claimed a large area: northeast Mississippi, northwest Alabama, west Tennessee, Kentucky, and even Ohio. Famed for their military skill, they courageously defended their wide-ranging territory. They were masters of the ambush and surprise attack. Today the Natchez Trace follows the old Chickasaw trading path.

The Creeks, populating a large area in what is today Georgia and Alabama, were a confederacy made up of many tribes, usually small. They banded together as protection from other tribes and from the encroaching white man. Members of the confederacy called themselves by the name of their individual tribe; for example, Chekilli (p. 23) called himself a Cussita. White people, however, unable to cope with so many groups, simply called these

Indians Creeks. First to join the core tribes of Muscogees were the Alibamos, Koasatis, and Hitchitis. The Apalachees, Shawnees, Yuchis, Natchez, and others came later. The Creeks managed to cling to their old ways in face of the intruding whites longer than any other southern tribe.

The Choctaws lived in Mississippi and west Alabama. A peace-loving people, they were noted as farmers and traders. The Choctaw language served as a basis for a trade language used across the South between Indians speaking several different languages and white people speaking several different European languages. Today about 5,000 Choctaws live in east central Mississippi on a reservation. Over 90 percent of these people still speak their native language.

The Seminoles formed much later than the other four great southern tribes. Various groups of Indians, mostly Creeks, fled to Florida in the late 1700s to escape wars and trouble with the white man. The story of the resistance of the Seminoles, "the wild (free) ones," to US Government efforts to drive them out of Florida became an epic in American history.

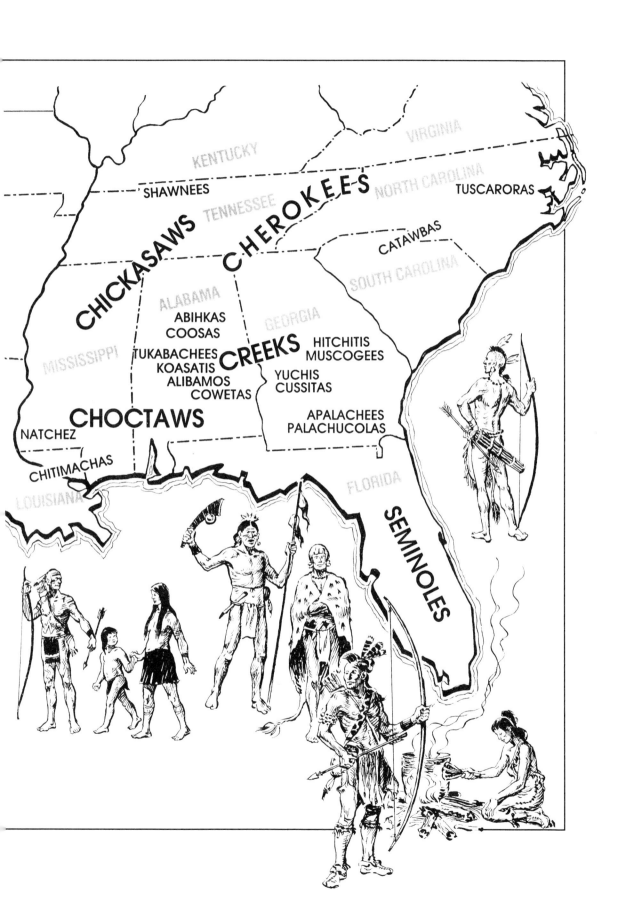

KENTUCKY

VIRGINIA

SHAWNEES

TENNESSEE

NORTH CAROLINA

TUSCARORAS

CHICKASAWS

CHEROKEES

CATAWBAS

SOUTH CAROLINA

ALABAMA

ABIHKAS
COOSAS

GEORGIA

HITCHITIS
MUSCOGEES

MISSISSIPPI

TUKABACHEES
KOASATIS
ALIBAMOS
COWETAS

CREEKS

YUCHIS
CUSSITAS

CHOCTAWS

APALACHEES
PALACHUCOLAS

NATCHEZ

CHITIMACHAS

LOUISIANA

FLORIDA

SEMINOLES

1

How the World Began

Southern Indians, like people all over the world, have many stories about the origins of the earth, about human and tribal beginnings.

In the beginning, they believed, water covered everything. Then a creature—the animal varies from tribe to tribe—brought up mud to make the earth. The Indians saw the earth as a flat surface; if they went to the edge of it, they could step off. The sky was a dome that fitted over the earth like an inverted bowl. The sky rose and fell at intervals; if one watched closely he could pass through the edges.

In telling about their own origins, the Indians say they came out of the earth, out of deep holes or caves, or hills or mountains. Several Creek tribes trace their beginning to the "navel" of the earth in the Rocky Mountains. Only the Yuchis and the Natchez claim direct descent from the sun.

Three stories in the section ("A Tribe Is Born," "The Long Journey," and "Panti Leads the Way") are known as migration legends. They tell of long treks from the west as Indian groups moved toward the rising sun, seeking their tribal identities and their homelands. In the Choctaw and Chickasaw legends, the people were led by a sacred pole; the pole became an important part of southern Indian rituals.

The Earth Is a Great Island

CHEROKEE

The earth is a great island floating in a sea of water. It is suspended at four points by cords hanging down from the sky vault, which is of solid rock. When the world grows old and worn out, the people will die and the cords will break and let the earth sink down into the ocean, and all will be water again. The Indians are afraid of this.

When all was water, the animals were in the Upper World, beyond the arch. But it was crowded, and they wanted more

room. The animals wondered what was below the water. At last Beaver's Grandchild, the little water beetle, offered to go to see if he could learn what was there. He darted in every direction over the surface of the water but could find no firm place to rest. Then he dived to the bottom and came up with some soft mud. Magically it began to grow and spread out in four directions. It became the island which we call the earth. It was afterward fastened to the sky with four cords, but no one remembers who did this.

At first the earth was flat and soft and wet. Eager to get down, the animals sent out different birds to see if the mud had dried. But the birds found no place to alight and came back to the Upper World. Then the animals sent the buzzard down. This was the great buzzard, the father of all the buzzards we see now. He flew all over the earth, low near the ground, and it was still soft. When he reached the Cherokee country he was very tired, and his wings began to flap and strike the ground. Whenever they struck the earth, a valley formed; and when they turned up, a mountain formed. When the animals above saw what the buzzard was doing, they were afraid the whole world would be mountains, so they called the buzzard back. But the Cherokee country is full of mountains to this day.

At last the earth was hard and dry, and the animals descended. It was dark, so they said to the sun, "Here's a road for you." They showed her the way to go, from east to west.

Now the animals had light, but it was too hot. The sun was too close to the earth. The red crawfish had his shell scorched a bright red, so that his meat was spoiled; and the Cherokees still do not eat it.

Everyone asked the medicine men to put the sun higher, but it was still too hot. They raised the sun another time, and another, until she was just under the sky arch. Then the sun was just right. Every day she goes along under this arch and returns at night to the starting place.

When the animals and plants were first made—we do not know by whom—they were told to watch and keep awake for seven nights, just as young men now fast and keep awake when they pray to their medicine. The animals and plants tried to do this, and nearly all were awake through the first night. But the next night several dropped off to sleep, and the third night others fell asleep. They kept falling asleep until, on the seventh night, only the owl and the mountain lion were still awake. To these two creatures was given the power to see in the dark, so they can hunt at night.

Of the trees only the cedar, the pine, the spruce, the holly, and the laurel were awake to the end. To them was given the ability always to be green and to be the greatest for medicine. To the other trees it was said, "Because you have not endured to the end, you shall lose your hair every winter."

Human beings were made after the animals and plants. At first there were only a brother and sister, until he poked her with a fish and told her to multiply. In seven days a child was born to her, and thereafter every seven days another. People increased so fast that there was danger the world could not keep them. Then it was arranged that a woman should have only one child in a year, and it has been so ever since.

This story was pieced together by James Mooney from many disjointed fragments; but Swimmer and John Ax were the main sources. Swimmer was the first and chief of storytellers, according to Mooney, who preserved the stories in Myths of the Cherokee. Born about 1835, Swimmer, whose real name was Ayunini, "grew up under the instruction of masters to be a priest, doctor, and keeper of tradition. "No green-corn dance, ballplay, or other tribal function was considered complete without his presence and active assistance. Proud of his people and their ancient system, he took delight in recording in his native alphabet the songs and sacred formulas of priests and dancers and the names of medicinal plants. His mind was a storehouse of Indian tradition. He had a musical voice and a faculty for imitating the characteristic cry of bird or beast. A photograph of Swimmer shows him wearing a turban and holding a gourd rattle, his badge of authority. He died in 1899. Mooney wrote: "Peace to his ashes and sorrow for his going, for with him perished half the tradition of a people."

When the Owl Hooted

ALIBAMO

The Alibamos came out of the ground near where the Alabama River and the Tombigbee River flow together. No sooner had they come out than an owl hooted. This scared them and most of them went back into the ground. That is why the Alibamos are few in number.

The Alibamos and their close cousins the Koasatis were among the first tribes to join the Creek Confederacy. In the 1830s they moved to south Texas and west Louisiana. An Alibamo living in Polk County, Texas, told this story to John R. Swanton. Communities of Alibamos live in that area today. The tribe gave its name to the state of Alabama.

A Tribe Is Born

CUSSITA

This speech, which has become the best-known southern Indian migration legend, was given by the Cussita chief Chekilli to the English governors at Savannah, Georgia, in 1735. Chekilli tells the story of his particular Creek tribe, the Cussita, from its ancient beginnings to its encounter with the peaceful Palachucola tribe. Tomochichi, chief of the Palachucolas at this time, was trying to persuade the Creeks to accept white settlers. He had been to London to sign a peace treaty.

At the end of the speech Chekilli expresses the dilemma of his people in signing a treaty with the whites. Yet, he says, Tomochichi's advice must be trusted. But the Creeks rapidly lost their land to the English after this meeting.

Chekilli's speech was written down on a buffalo skin by a Creek interpreter who handed it over to the English at the Savannah meeting. From there it went to London to hang in the Colony of Georgia offices in Westminster. That copy was lost. But over one hundred years later the anthropologist Albert Gatschet discovered a copy in German, made for a group of Germans migrating to the Georgia colony in 1741. "A Tribe Is Born" is a paraphrase of most of Gatschet's translation of the German copy of Chekilli's speech.

A long time ago the Cussitas came out of the navel of the earth in the Rocky Mountains and set out to the east looking for their homeland. They were also looking for their fire and for their medicine.

As they journeyed they heard a noise like thunder. They sent people ahead to find out what it was.

"It is a mountain that thunders," the scouts reported. "And red smoke belches from it."

The Cussitas approached the mountain and found three other groups there: the Chickasaws, the Alibamos, and the Abihkas, who were also very young and had no fire or medicine.

They all heard singing on the mountain and climbed to see what it was. They found a great fire that blazed and sang. "The fire has been given to us," the people said.

Later more fire came to them from four directions. From the east came a white fire which they would not use. From the south came a blue fire; neither would they use it. From the west came a black fire; nor would they use it. At last came a fire from the north, which was red and yellow. This they mingled with the fire from the mountain. And it became the sacred fire from which all other fires were lit.

The people named the mountain the King of Mountains. It thunders to this day, and people are afraid of it.

HOW MEDICINE CAME   After they left the mountain, the people again heard singing. This time it was herbs and roots singing about their benefits. The people realized they had found the medicine for which they had been waiting. First they were given the p*asa,* button snakeroot; next, the *miko hoyanidja,* the redroot; then, the *sowatcka,* like wild fennel; and fourth, h*itchi laputcki,* like tobacco.

HOW WAR STARTED   A dispute arose as to which of the groups was the oldest nation and which should rule. Since the people now had fire and medicine to help them, they decided to settle the dispute by going to war and collecting scalps. They set up four red poles, one for each nation. The nation that covered the pole first from top to bottom with scalps would be the oldest.

The Cussitas covered their pole first, so thickly that it was hidden from sight. Therefore they were looked upon by the whole nation as the oldest. The Chickasaws covered their pole next, then the Alibamos. But the Abihkas could cover their pole only as high as the knee.

KILLING THE MONSTER BIRD   A big bird, blue in color with a long tail and swifter than an eagle, began to prey on the people. He came every day and ate some of them.

The nations held a council and decided to try to trick the bird. They made a figure in the shape of a woman and put it in the path where the bird would see it. They hoped the bird would take it to be his mate.

The bird came and carried the figure away. Then, after a long time he brought it back. The people left it alone and watched it, hoping their trick had worked and that something would come out of it.

After a time, a red rat came from the figure. The people believed that the bird was the father of the rat, and that the rat would know how to kill the bird. So they discussed it with the rat.

"The bird carries a bow and arrows to defend himself," said the rat. "I will gnaw the bowstring in two." He did this, and the people were able to kill the great bird, which they named King of Birds.

The people think the eagle also is a great king. They carry its feathers when they go to war or make peace. The red feathers mean war, the white, peace. If an enemy approaches with white feathers and a white mouth, and cries like an eagle, they dare not kill him.

THE MAN-EATER LION OF COOSA   Now the four nations continued journeying toward the sunrise, led by the Cussitas. They came to a town and a people called Coosa. The Coosas complained that they were being attacked by a man-eating lion that lived in a cave. The Cussitas said they would try to kill the animal.

They dug a pit and stretched over it a net made of hickory bark. Then they laid branches crosswise so the lion could not follow them.

Going to his den, they threw a rattle of turtle shells inside the cave. The lion rushed out angrily and chased them and fell in the pit. The Cussitas threw the net over the lion and killed him with blazing pine wood.

The lion's bones are preserved to this day. When the Cussitas go to war, they take the lion's bones with them as part of their war medicine. The bones bring them good luck.

PEOPLE OF THE WHITE PATH   The Cussitas came to a white footpath. The grass and everything around were white, indicating that people had been there. The Cussitas wanted to find out who the people were. They believed the white path might be the path for them to follow.

They walked along the path to a river, where they came to a waterfall. On some big rocks they saw bows lying. And they believed the people who made the white path had been there. So the Cussitas sent ahead two scouts. The scouts climbed a high mountain and saw a town. They shot arrows into the town, but the people of the town shot back red arrows, so the scouts knew they were not the people of the white path.

Later the Cussitas came again to a white path and saw the smoke of a town. They had found at last the people they had been seeking. The town was the place where now the tribe of Palachucolas live, from whom Tomochichi is descended.

THE CUSSITAS SETTLE DOWN   The Cussitas liked to fight, but the Palachucolas gave them black drink as a sign of friendship, and said, "Our hearts are white, and yours must be white. You must lay down the bloody tomahawk and show your bodies as a proof that they shall be white." The Palachucolas persuaded the Cussitas to give up the tomahawk, and they buried their weapons under their beds. The Palachucolas also gave them white feathers. And they asked to have a chief in common. Since then the two people have always lived together.

Some settled on one side of the river, some on the other. Those on one side are called Cussitas, those on the other, Cowetas. Yet they are one people.

Still, as the Cussitas first saw the red smoke and the red fire, and live in war towns, they cannot yet leave their read hearts— which actually are white on one side and red on the other. The Cussitas now know that the white path was the best for them. Although Tomochichi was a stranger, they see he has done them good, because he went to see the great king with Esquire Oglethorpe and hear his talk, and related it to them, and they listened to it and believed it.

To the Creeks the colors red and white stood for war and peace. Creek towns were either war, or red, towns; or peace, or white, towns. The war towns organized war parties, led raiding expeditions, and took care of ceremonies related to war. The white towns had the responsibility of carrying out ceremonies not related to war, such as the green corn ceremony or ball games.

Colors had special meanings among the other southern tribes, too. For the Cherokees red paint was symbolic of war, strength, success, and spirit protection. One of the Cherokees' seven clans was the Paint clan.

Children of the Sun

YUCHI

In the beginning waters covered everything. Someone said, "Who will make the land appear?" Lock-chew, the crawfish, said, "I will make the land appear." He went to the bottom of the water and began to stir up the mud with his tail and hands. He brought the mud to the surface and piled it up.

The beings who lived at the bottom of the water said, "Who is disturbing our land?" They kept watch and discovered the crawfish. When they approached him, he suddenly stirred the mud with his tail so they could not see him.

Lock-chew continued carrying mud and piling it up until at last he held up his hands in the air, and land appeared above the water.

The land was soft. Someone said, "Who will spread out the land and make it dry and hard?" Another said, "Ahyok, the hawk, should spread out the soft land and make it dry." Others said, "Yah-tee, the buzzard, has larger wings. He can spread out the land and make it dry and hard."

Yah-tee undertook to spread out and dry the earth. He flew above the earth and spread out his long wings over it. But after awhile he grew tired of holding out his wings and began to flap them. In this way he caused the hills and valleys, because the dirt was still soft as he flapped his wings.

"Who will make the light?" someone said. It was dark.

Yo-hah, the star, said, "I will make the light."

Everyone agreed, and the star shone forth. But it was light only near the star.

"Who will make more light?" someone asked.

Shar-pah, the moon, said, "I will make more light." Shar-pah made more light, but it was still dark.

An influential tribe, the Yuchis were one of the last groups to become a part of the Creek Confederacy. They took pride in observing their own tribal customs, however, and did not mix well in the confederacy. Descendants of these people meet once a year in Columbus, Georgia, to take part in a tribal celebration.

This story was told by a Yuchi to William O. Tuggle around 1880.

T-cho, the sun, said, "You are my children. I am your mother. I will make the light. I will shine for you."

The sun went to the east. Suddenly light spread over all the earth. As the sun passed over the earth a drop of blood fell from her to the ground. From this blood and earth sprang the first people, the children of the sun, the Yuchis.

Nanih Waiya, Mother Mound

CHOCTAW

A long time ago, people were created at the mount called Nanih Waiya. First to come out of the mound were the Muscogees. They sunned themselves on the earthen rampart, and when they got dry they traveled to the east. By the Tombigbee River they rested. While smoking tobacco they dropped some fire.

The Cherokees next came out of Nanih Waiya. They also sunned themselves on the earthen rampart, and when they got dry they followed the trail of the older tribe. At the place where the Muscogees had stopped and rested, and where they had smoked tobacco, a fire had burned the woods. The Cherokees could not find the Muscogees' trail. So they trekked to the north where they settled and made a homeland.

The Chickasaws came third out of Nanih Waiya. They sunned themselves on the earthen rampart. When they got dry they followed the Cherokees' trail and settled close to the Cherokees.

The Choctaws came fourth and last out of Nanih Waiya. They sunned themselves on the earthen rampart, and when they got dry they did not go anywhere but settled down on the spot.

And this land is the Choctaws' home.

This is a Choctaw explanation of the origin of the main southern tribes. The Muscogees were the original tribe making up the Creek Confederacy.

Nanih Waiya is a real place in Mississippi where today one may visit the great mound.

Isaac Pistonatubbee, a Mississippi Choctaw, told this story to Henry Halbert about 1870. Halbert took the story down word for word in Choctaw and then translated it.

The Origin of Races

Listen and I will tell you how the Master of Life made man.

After the world was made it was very beautiful. The forests abounded in game and fruit. The great plains were covered with deer and elk and buffalo. The rivers were full of fish. There were many bears and beavers and other fat animals. But there was no human being to enjoy these things.

Then the Master of Life said, "We will make man."

Man was made, but when he stood before his maker, he was white. The Master of Life was sorry. He saw that the being he had made was pale and weak.

The Master of Life tried again, for he was determined to make a perfect man. But in his effort to make a perfect man, he went to the opposite extreme: when the second human being stood before him, he was black. The Master of Life liked the black man less than the white, and he shoved him aside to make room for another try.

Then it was that he made the red man. And the red man pleased him.

This popular myth has several versions among the Seminoles and Creeks. In other tellings, the Master of Breath molds man in clay form and bakes him: the white man too little, the black too much, and the red man just right.

Chief Neamathla told this version to William Duvall, governor of Florida, in 1842. Neamathla bitterly opposed US Government efforts to teach Seminole children the ways of the white people. He shocked Washington by refusing a payment of one thousand dollars to build a school for this purpose. He said, "We wish our children to remain as the Master of Life made them, and as their fathers are, Indians."

The Long Journey
CHOCTAW

In ancient times the ancestors of the Choctaws and Chickasaws lived in a country far away in the west. They lived in two clans and were ruled by two brothers, Chahta and Chikasa.

As time passed, so many people were born that the land could no longer support them. There was not enough food to eat.

The people looked for help to a great prophet. He told them: "We must leave this land and make our way far to the east. There we will find a country with fertile soil and game of all kinds."

The people prepared for the long journey. They marched by clan, with seven days' difference in their departing times.

The great prophet marched at the head of the first group, carrying a long pole. When camp was made each night, he planted the pole upright in front of the camp.

"The pole will tell us which way to go," he said.

First the pole leaned to the north, and the people went in that direction. The journey led across streams, over mountains, through forests and barren prairies. The people always followed the direction in which the pole pointed each morning.

They had traveled a great distance when they came to the banks of O-kee-na-chitto, the great waterway (Mississippi River). They camped for the night and the prophet planted the pole.

The next morning the pole leaned east, across the river.

"We must build rafts and cross the great river," the prophet said. So the people felled trees and made a thousand rafts to cross on.

When they reached the other side they found a beautiful country, with green forests and streams. There was game of every kind and abundant fruits and flowers. "This surely is the end of our journey," the people said. "Let us settle here." But the pole still leaned to the east.

At last the people came to a great mound and made camp beside it. The next morning they were awakened by the shouts of the prophet: "The pole stands straight. We have found our country. This mound is the center of our land." The mound came to be known as Nanih Waiya.

As it so happened, the group led by Chikasa had crossed a creek further east and camped on its bank. During the night a great rain began to fall. It lasted several days and the creek flooded the low-lying land where Chikasa and his clan had camped.

When the rains stopped, Chahta sent a messenger to tell Chikasa that the long-sought land had been found. But the Chikasa clan had proceeded on their jourrney. The rain had washed away all the trace of them. Chahta's messenger had to return with the news that his brother could not be found.

Chikasa's group moved on to the Tombigbee River and eventually became a separate nation. In this way the Choctaws and the Chickasaws became two separate, though related, nations.

Peter Folsom, a Choctaw living in the western Indian Territory, came in 1882 as a Baptist missionary to the Mississippi Choctaws. In telling this story to H.S. Halbert, Folsom said his father had told it to him when the two visited Nanih Waiya together in 1883.

Panti Leads the Way

CHICKASAW

The earliest home of the Indian people was the continent of Asia. After a time they got tired of living there and wanted to move to a place where they could live in comfort, have a country of their own, and be independent.

It was revealed to them that they must move toward the east, so they set out in that direction. They had a dog named Panti who guarded their camp at night and kept the wild animals away. He walked in advance to direct them. He led them out of difficulties and kept them from getting into places from which they might not be able to escape. If anyone was bitten by a snake, Panti would lick the wound and the person would get well.

The people kept moving eastward until they came to a big body of water which they called Ok-hata (Big Ocean). They camped on the shore of this big water. Seeing land on the other side, the people decided to cross over. They held councils to decide how to accomplish this.

They built a raft, but after they had finished it they discovered they could cross only at certain times when the water moved back. At last they crossed safely to North America, but it was so cold there that they started on again southward until they came to Montana, where they remained a long time.

At the end of that period they held a council. Some wanted to move on, while others preferred to stay. So they divided. Those who wished to leave took the dog Panti with them as their guide. They loved him dearly, for he was a great help to them.

Moving eastward, they came to a prairie where they found many wild animals, some of which Panti killed for the people to eat, while he drove the rest away. There were plenty of deer, prairie chickens, turkeys, squirrels, fish, and other creatures good to eat. There were also some dangerous animals, such as panthers and wolves. But the people moved along cautiously so that these creatures could not get at them.

Whenever they decided to move, they began several days in advance to prepare food for the journey: blue or shuck bread and cold flour.

When they reached the Mississippi River they camped on its banks for some time, uncertain how they could get to the other side. Finally they built a raft. But during the crossing their raft came to pieces and their faithful dog Panti was lost.

After this sad event the people at first did not know what to do. Finally they decided to use a wooden pole as their guide. It would tell them in which direction to march. The pole led them eventually to Chikasaw Old Fields, where they settled.

Another version of the Chickasaw migration legend says the great dog was lost in Mississippi. The Chickasaws always believed that the dog fell into a large sinkhole. They could hear the dog howl just before nightfall. Whenever their warriors got scalps, they gave them to the boys to throw into the sinkhole. After throwing the scalps, the boys would run off in fright; if one of them fell while running, the Chickasaws were sure he would be killed or taken captive by an enemy.

The Panti story, obviously influenced by the modern theory of how the Indians reached North America, was told by Zeno Mc-Curtain, a Chickasaw interpreter, to John R. Swanton. Ok-hata (Big Ocean) must be the Bering Strait. The original Chickasaw Old Fields was located on the Tennessee River east of present-day Muscle Shoals in Alabama.

Oka Falama, the Great Flood

CHOCTAW

In ancient times, people became so wicked that the Great Spirit decided to destroy the human race. He sent a prophet to go from tribe to tribe and village to village to warn the people that they soon would be destroyed. But no one believed the prophet.

Then, cloudy days and nights came, when the sun and moon and stars could not be seen. After that came total darkness. The sun seemed to have been blotted out. The people heard mutterings of thunder in the distance, gradually becoming louder and closer until the noise reverberated all over the sky. Fear and consternation seized the people, and the wise men sang death songs.

People had to use torchlight to get from place to place. Food became moldy and unfit to eat. The wild animals of the forest gathered around the village fires, bewildered.

Suddenly a fearful crash of thunder, louder than had ever been heard, seemed to shake the earth. Immediately afterward the people saw a glimmering light far away to the north. Hopeful at first, they soon realized the light was not that of the returning sun, but the gleam of huge, billowing waters.

"Oka falama, oka falama (waters returning)," the people wailed as wave after wave swept over the land and destroyed everything. Soon the earth was entirely covered by the rushing water. Only one person was saved: the mysterious prophet who had been sent by the Great Spirit to warn of approaching doom.

The prophet saved himself by making a raft of sassafras logs. As he floated on the waters, various kinds of fish swam around him, and twined among the branches of the submerged trees he could see bodies of people and animals.

After many weeks of floating, the prophet spotted a large black bird flying in circles over his raft. The prophet called to the bird for help, but the bird only croaked and flew away.

A few days later a bird of bluish color, with red eyes and beak, hovered over the raft. "Is there a spot of dry land anywhere to be seen?" the prophet called out.

The bird flew around the prophet's head, crying mournfully, and then flew in the direction where the new sun seemed to be sinking into the great ocean of waters. A strong wind sprang up and blew the raft in that direction.

The next day the prophet sighted an island in the distance. The raft drifted toward it and by nightfall the prophet landed on the island and encamped. Weary and lonely, he forgot his anxieties in sleep. In the morning, he found the island covered with all kinds of animals and birds, among which was the bird which had visited him on the waters and left him to his fate. The prophet named him the crow. To the Choctaws, the crow has always been a bird of bad luck.

With great joy he also discovered the bird which had caused the wind to blow his raft toward the island. Because of this act of kindness, and because of the bird's great beauty, the prophet called her Puchi Yushuba (Lost Pigeon, or turtle dove).

After many days, the water receded. In the course of time Puchi Yushuba became a beautiful woman, whom the prophet married, and by them the world was again peopled.

Living on river deltas, the early southern Indians experienced periodic floods and told many stories about a great flood. This story was recorded by H. B. Cushman, a missionary who lived almost all of his life with the Choctaws and who wrote A History of the Choctaw, Chickasaw, and Natchez Indians *(1899).*

2

Gifts of the Great Spirit

Southern Indians believed that certain things such as corn, fire, and medicine came to them as gifts from a supreme being.

The supreme being had several names among the southern tribes. The Creeks and Seminoles called him the Master of Breath, Breath-maker, and the Master of Life. To the Choctaws he was Beloved One Above, and to the Chickasaws, Big Holy One Above. To the Cherokees he was Yowa, a name used only by medicine men. The term Great Spirit for the Indians' supreme deity was first used by the white man.

Stories about the gifts from the supreme being are among the sacred myths of the tribes, their telling usually reserved for medicine men or myth-keepers.

Rabbit Steals Fire

CREEK

In ancient times there was no fire. It existed only on the other side of the ocean to the east.

The people came together and said, "How shall we obtain fire?"

Big Man-eater said, "I can bring it." So he started off. He jumped into the ocean. But he was never seen again.

Rabbit said, "I can bring the fire. No one else knows how, but I know how to bring it back."

So he started off. When he got to the ocean, he pulled off his shirt and threw it down. He placed wooden sticks on it. Then he sat on it and crossed the water.

The people who had the fire welcomed Rabbit and gave a great dance to celebrate his coming.

Rabbit entered the dancing circle wearing a cap into which he had stuck four sticks of pine resin. The dancers danced nearer and nearer the sacred fire in the center of the circle. Rabbit danced nearer and nearer the fire. The dancers bowed lower and lower to the sacred fire. Rabbit also bowed lower and lower to the fire.

Suddenly, as he bent very low, the sticks of resin caught fire. His head burst into flame.

When the people saw what had happened, they cried, "He has dared to touch the sacred fire. Catch him." They grabbed at Rabbit.

But Rabbit ran away, with the people chasing him. When he got to the great water, he plunged in and swam away from the people, who could only watch from the shore.

Rabbit swam all the way across the ocean with the flames blazing from his cap and returned to his people and gave them the fire.

After the people had gotten fire from across the ocean, they were forbidden to build a fire except in the busk (ceremonial) ground. It was customary to build a fire whenever there was to be a dance.

Rabbit heard about the dance and thought, "I will steal fire from the busk ground."

This time he rubbed his head with pine resin to make his hair stand up. Then he went down to the busk ground where many people had gathered. When they saw Rabbit they said, "You must lead the dance."

Rabbit agreed. He began singing as he danced around the fire, with many people following him. They all danced harder and harder as Rabbit circled closer and closer to the fire.

Suddenly he poked his head into the fire. His head blazed up, and Rabbit ran. The people shouted, "Hulloa! Catch him."

"Rabbit Steals Fire" is based on stories told to John R. Swanton by members of the Hitchiti and Koasati tribes in the early 1900s.

The Hitchitis, one of the oldest tribes in the Creek Confederacy, were living in the Macon, Georgia, area when the English first came. Later some of the Hitchitis moved into Florida, becoming Seminoles. They spoke the ancient Hitchiti, a language distinct from the Muskogean. The Koasatis lived with the Alibamos along the Alabama River and joined the Creek Confederacy. In the Removal they settled in west Louisiana and south Texas.

But Rabbit disappeared.

The people made it rain for four days. "That is long enough to put out the fire that Rabbit has stolen," they said.

But Rabbit had built a fire in a hollow tree and stayed there while it rained. When the rain stopped, he came out and set fires all around. Again it rained, and the fires were put out. But Rabbit again built a fire inside a hollow tree. The next time the rain stopped and Rabbit set fires all around, the people took the fires and ran off with them.

This is how Rabbit stole fire from the busk ground and scattered it so all the people could have fire.

How Bears Lost Fire
ALIBAMO

 Bears in ancient times owned Fire and always took him about with them. One time they put Fire on the ground while they foraged nearby for acorns.

Fire almost went out and called aloud, "Feed me."

Some people heard him. "What do you want to eat?" they asked.

"I want to eat wood."

The people got a stick from the north and laid it down on Fire. They got a stick from the west and laid it also on Fire. They got a stick from the south and laid it on Fire. They got a stick from the east and laid it on Fire.

Fire blazed up.

When the bears came back to get their Fire, Fire said, "I don't know you any more. I belong to human beings."

Water Spider's Tusti Bowl

CHEROKEE

In the beginning there was no fire, and the world was cold.

Then the Thunders, who lived up in Galunlati, sent their lightning and put fire in the bottom of a hollow sycamore tree on an island.

The animals knew fire was there, because they could see the smoke coming out at the top of the tree, but they could not get to it because of the water. They held a council to decide what to do.

Every animal that could fly or swim was eager to go after the fire. Raven offered, and because he was so large and strong the animals thought he could surely do the work. So he was sent first. He flew high and far across the water and alighted on the sycamore tree, but while he was wondering what to do next, the heat scorched his feathers black. He was frightened and came back without the fire.

Little Screech Owl volunteered to go. He reached the trees safely, but while he was looking down into the hollow tree a blast of hot air came up and nearly burned out his eyes. He managed to fly home, but it was a long time before he could see well. His eyes are red to this day.

Then Hooting Owl and Horned Owl went. by the time they got to the hollow tree the fire was burning so fiercely that the smoke nearly blinded them, and the ashes carried up by the wind made white rings about their eyes. They had to come home without the fire. With all their rubbing they were never able to get rid of the white rings.

No more of the birds would venture to the burning tree. But the little snake, Black Racer, said he would go and bring back fire. He swam across to the island and crawled through the grass to the tree, which he entered through a small hole. The heat and the smoke were too much for him, too, and after dodging about blindly over the hot ashes, he managed to get out the hole by which he had entered. But his body had been scorched black, and ever since he has had the habit of darting and doubling on his track as if trying to escape from close quarters

After Black Racer came back, the great snake, Black Climber, offered to go for fire. He swam over to the island and climbed up the tree on the outside, as the climber always does. but when he put his head down into the hole, the smoke choked him so that he fell into the burning stump. Before he could climb out again he was as black as Black Racer.

The animals held another council, for still there was no fire and the world was still cold. Birds, snakes, and four-footed animals all had some excuse for not going to the island, because they were all afraid to venture near the burning sycamore.

At last Water Spider said she would go. Water Spider has black downy hair and red stripes on her body. She can run on top of the water or dive to the bottom, so she would have no trouble getting to the island. But the question was, how could she bring back the fire?

"I'll manage that," said Water Spider. She spun a thread from her body and wove it into a *tusti* bowl which she fastened on her back. Then she crossed over to the island and moved through the grass to the burning tree.

Water Spider put one little coal of fire into her bowl, and she came back to the animals with it.

Ever since, we have had fire. And Water Spider still keeps her *tusti* bowl.

Grandmother and the Orphan Boy

CREEK

An old woman who lived alone found a drop of blood in a puddle of rainwater. She laid the drop of blood aside carefully and covered it. Sometime later she removed the cover and found a baby under it.

The woman took care of the orphan boy. He called her his grandmother. She made a bow and arrows for him when he was about four feet tall, and he began hunting. She warned him not to go to a big mountain in the distance.

The first time the boy came back from hunting, he said to his grandmother, "What is the thing with a blue head?"

"It is a turkey. We can eat it. Kill it."

The next time the boy came home he said, "What is the thing with a white tail?"

"It is a deer. Go and kill it."

In this way the boy learned the names of animals that were good to hunt for food.

Whenever the boy got back from hunting, his grandmother had prepared a delicious dinner of dumplings or hominy or another corn dish. They boy wondered where she got the corn.

One day, instead of going hunting, he slipped back to the cabin and peeped through a crack. He saw his grandmother place a pot on the floor, stand with her feet on either side of it, and scratch her thighs. When she did this, corn poured from her body into the pot. "So that is how she gets the corn," the boy said to himself.

The next time the boy came back from hunting, he could not eat the hominy his grandmother put before him. "What is the matter?" she said. "Are you sick?"

The boy shook his head and turned his back.

"Ah," his grandmother said, "you must have spied on me. You know how I get the corn. If you do not want to eat the food I prepare, you must go beyond the mountain I forbade you to pass over.

"But before you leave, go and hunt birds for me."

They boy killed some birds and brought them to his grandmother.

"Bring another kind," she said.

So he went off again and killed other birds.

"Bring yet another kind," she said.

They boy tried again. Finally he brought jaybirds.

"These are the ones," his grandmother said. "Now bring me some rattlesnakes."

After he had done this, his grandmother brought the birds and snakes back to life. She made the youth a headdress of bluejays and rattlesnakes. Then she made him a flute. When he played it all the birds sang and the snakes shook their rattles.

"Now," said the grandmother, "all is ready for you to go to the mountain. But before you leave, you must do one more thing. Lock me up in this cabin and set fire to it.

"After you have been gone for some time, and have a wife, come back to this place where you grew up."

The youth set fire to the cabin as his grandmother had directed and started down the path that led to the mountain. When he had crossed over the mountain he found some people playing ball, among them Rabbit. They all stopped to look at the youth and admire his headdress of bluejays and rattlesnakes.

When Rabbit saw how much the people admired the youth, he was jealous and wanted to be like him. So Rabbit persuaded the youth to let him travel along with him.

Before they had gone far, they came to a pond. "There are many turtles here," Rabbit said. "Let's go down into the water and get a lot of them."

The youth agreed. They took off their clothes and put them under a tree. Rabbit said, "When I shout, 'All ready,' we will dive in." The boy dived in, but Rabbit ran back to the tree, took the youth's headdress and flute, and went off with them.

The youth traveled on alone. He found some people who liked him even without his headdress and flute. He was staying with these people when word came that Rabbit had been arrested for stealing his possessions.

The youth went to reclaim his headdress and flute. The bluejays and the snakes, who had been silent while they were with Rabbit, began singing and rattling with joy when they saw the youth again. He put on his headdress, took his flute, and returned to the people who had taken him in.

He found a young woman among these people, and he married her. He said to his wife, "Let us go down to the creek. I want to swim. By crossing the creek four times I can kill all the fish there."

His wife agreed, and he went swimming and killed all the fish. He told his wife to call her people together. They all came and had a great meal of fish.

When Rabbit heard what the youth had done, he wanted to imitate him. Rabbit said to his wife, "Let us go down to the creek. I want to swim. When I cross four times the fish will come to the surface."

"Well, go and do it," his wife said.

So Rabbit swam across the creek four times. When he dived he struck a minnow and stunned it. When he came out of the water, he saw the minnow floating as if it had been poisoned. Rabbit told his wife to call her people to come get fish. She did so, but when they came they found only one minnow at the edge of the water. They returned home very angry with Rabbit.

Sometime later, the youth remembered what his grandmother had told him. He said to his wife, "Let us go over the mountain to the place where I grew up." So they went. They found the spot covered with corn plants.

That is how the Indians got corn. The grandmother was corn.

Stories about the origin of corn and hunting, two main sources of food, appear more often and in more versions than any other southern Indian myth.

The southern Indians were good farmers and corn was their most important crop. Corn was roasted or boiled while green, parched and pounded into meal when dry. Sofkee mush, dumplings, hominy, succotash, all were made from corn. Moccasins, masks, and dolls were made from cornhusks. Corncob fires, almost smokeless, heated houses. Village life centered around the planting and harvesting of corn. Corn also figured in sacred rites, the most important of which was the green corn ceremony, taking place in summer when the corn had ripened. The green corn celebration ended when a priest started a new fire. His first act was to place four ears of ripe corn in the fire, an offering of thanksgiving to the Breathmaker for another year.

How Koonti Came

SEMINOLE

 The Breath-maker took seven men on a long walk. In fact, they traveled down from Georgia to a place a little below Miami

While they rested there the seven men became hungry, and the Breath-maker taught them how to fish. He also dug into the ground just a few feet from the ocean until water sprang up. Then the Breath-maker made it rain, and he told his companions to go outside.

They found the ground covered with little cakes.

The next morning the Breath-maker made the little cakes sprout roots from their sides. This was the koonti plant.

Koonti root is like a turnip in appearance but larger. Seminole women removed the skin and pounded it into flour for breadmaking, using it as a substitute for cornmeal.

This story was told by a Seminole medicine man, Ko-nip-hat-co, to his son Panther (Josie Billie), who in turn told it to Robert F. Greenlee in 1939.

The Unknown Woman
CHOCTAW

Two Choctaw hunters camped for the night on a bend in the Alabama River. They were tired and discouraged, having hunted for two days and killed only one black hawk. They had no game to take back to their village.

While they were roasting the hawk on the campfire for their supper, they heard a low, plaintive sound like the call of a dove. The sad notes broke the deep night silence again and again. As the full moon rose across the river, the strange sound became more distinct.

The men looked up and down the river but saw only the sandy shore in the moonlight. Then they looked in the opposite direction and to their astonishment saw a beautiful woman dressed in white, standing on a mound. She beckoned to the hunters.

"I am very hungry," the woman said.

One of the hunters ran to the campfire and brought the roasted hawk to the woman. After she had eaten some, she gave the rest back to them. "You have saved me from death. I will not forget your kindness.

"One full moon from now, in midsummer," she continued, "return to the mound where I am standing."

Suddenly a gentle breeze came up, and the woman disappeared

as mysteriously as she had come.

The hunters knew they had seen Unknown Woman, daughter of the Great Spirit.

They returned to their village but kept secret the strange meeting with the woman.

One month later, when the moon was full, the hunters came to the place where Unknown Woman had spoken to them. As the moon rose over the opposite bank they stood at the foot of the mound, waiting. But Unknown Woman was nowhere to be seen.

"She has not come as she promised," they said to each other.

Then one hunter remembered. "She told us to come to the very spot where she stood." So the men climbed the mound. They could not believe what they saw: the mound was covered with a plant they had never seen. It was a tall plant with leaves like knives and delicate tassels emerging from the spike-like fruit, or ears. Inside the ears was a delicious food.

So it was that the Choctaws received the gift of *tanchi*, corn. They cultivated corn ever afterward and never again were hungry.

Thunder Boys

NATCHEZ

Long ago a hunter took his son to stay with him at the hunting camp. One day when the father got ready to go hunting, his son said, "Make some arrows and leave them with me."

The hunter left the arrows with him, but the next day his son again asked for arrows.

"How do you use up so many arrows?" the father asked.

"A wild boy comes around and we shoot together," the boy said. "We bet and he wins all my arrows."

"When he comes back, you must catch him. I will help you."

So the father made more arrows and left the camp. But he stayed nearby, watching. When the wild boy came, the son began to wrestle with him as his father told him to do. Then the father ran up to them and tied up Wild Boy before he could get away.

The hunter kept Wild Boy tied up until he was sure he wouldn't try to run away. He decided to keep him as his second boy. One day he thought it safe to leave the boys together and go hunting. He said to them:

"Today someone from the west will call to you to be ferried across the creek in a canoe. This is not a human being but Old-Woman-Who-Sticks-to-You. You must not take her across.

"When someone shouts to you from the east, that will be a human being, and you can take that one across."

No sooner had the hunter left than someone shouted to them from the west, "Boys, come take me across."

"Let's go get her," Wild Boy said.

"But Father said not to take her across, that she is not a human being."

"If you do not do it, I will hack you with Father's big ax."

That frightened Tame Boy so much that he agreed to go along.

The two boys ferried Old-Woman-Who-Sticks-to-You across the creek in the canoe. They were jumping up the slippery bank

when she leaped after them and fastened herself onto them. They tried to get her off, but she stuck fast. Finally they had to kill her and pour boiling water over her to get unstuck. They cut off her nose and made a pipe out of it. "It will be good for Father to use when he smokes," they said

When their father came home, he said, "Have you been right here while I've been gone?"

"We've been nowhere else. And we have made a pipe for you."

He put tobacco in it, lighted it, and smoked. Then he said, "Didn't you do what I told you not to do?"

Tame Boy answered, "We put Old-Woman-Who-Sticks-to-You across the creek and jumped back, but she jumped back too and stuck to us. When we could do nothing else with her we killed her."

The next time the father started out to hunt he said to the boys, "If you want to go swimming you must not swim in the creek to the west. You must swim to the east. There are leeches in the creek to the west."

Soon after he left, the boys decided to go swimming. They swam on the east side of the creek. Then Wild Boy said, "Let's go find out about the leeches."

"Father forbade us," said Tame Boy.

"If you won't go I'll hack you with Father's ax," said Wild Boy. So Tame Boy agreed to go, and they went swimming on the west side of the creek.

When they came out, leeches were all over their bodies. They wallowed in the sand and mashed them.

When their father came home he said, "Have you been right here?" Wild Boy answered, "We have been nowhere else."

But Tame Boy said, "We went swimming where you said not to. When we came out, leeches hung all over us. We rolled in the sand and mashed them, and when their skins were dried they made a noise—sgakak, sgakak. And we danced."

Later, the two boys agreed that the next time their father left to hunt they would follow him. They made themselves many arrows and hid them from their father. When the father left, the boys followed. They kept just out of sight so their father would not know he was being followed.

When the hunter came to a high mountain, he opened a door at the foot of it, and out came a deer which he shot and killed. He shut the door, laid the deer on his back, and started home.

The boys came out of their hiding place, and when they were sure their father had gone they opened the door in the mountain. All kinds of animals—deer and turkeys and bear—ran out. The boys shot at them until they ran out of arrows. Then they started whooping and clapping their hands, trying to get the animals to go back into the mountain. But the animals had scattered in all directions. So the boys shut the door and ran home, getting there before their father.

When he arrived he said, "Have you been off anywhere?"

And they answered, "We have been here all the time."

When the deer meat gave out and the father again started off to hunt, he could find no game. He came home and said, "You are the ones who let the animals out. That food was for us to live on. We must go back to the settlement where I came from." So all three set out.

When they reached the settlement, the father said, "I want to look around," and he went off. In the evening he came back and told the boys he was going to a council meeting, and he left again.

The boys decided to follow him to the meeting. They saw people gathering outside the council house, and when it was dark, the people went in. The boys crept under the floor to hear what was going on. They heard that they themselves were being tried for letting out the animals. The people were very angry because now they would have to hunt for game scattered over the earth.

The boys were convicted. The council decided to kill the boys before morning.

The boys wasted no time preparing to protect themselves. They knew the people would be coming after them. They hid

In the beginning, men did not have to hunt for game. Deer and other animals came as a gift like corn and tobacco. People could open a door and game would come out. Then along came two unruly boys, showoffs with no respect for authority, and the picture changed forever

In some Creek and Cherokee stories Tame Boy is called Lodge Boy, because he lived in a lodge, and Wild Boy is called Thrown-Away Boy, because he was an orphan.

in a small corncrib. They stationed guards at four points to let them know when the people got close to the corncrib. The guards farthest away were ducks. At the next station were geese; at the next, sandhill cranes, and closest to the crib were quail.

The boys then filled four hollow canes with four kinds of stinging insects: bumblebees, hornets, yellow jackets, wasps.

They sat in the corncrib, waiting and ready.

The ducks flew past. "I think they are coming," said one of the boys. After awhile, the geese went by. "They are getting closer." After another interval the sandhill cranes flew over. "They are almost here." Still later, the quail flew past. "They have come!"

At that instant the boys opened the hollow canes and threw them out at the people. The insects stung them so badly that in trying to fight them off the people struck and killed one another.

Towards daylight the shouting and tumult quieted down. The stinging insects flew away. So the boys came out of the corncrib. The people lay about, dead.

"What shall we do?" the boys said.

"We will go into the ground."

"No, for we could never see each other."

"Then, let us wade into the water."

"If we do that we shall not be able to see each other."

Then they said, "If we go above, we can be together."

So they went up into the sky and became the Thunder Boys. When they talk to each other, we hear rolling thunder.

Told by Watt Sam of Oklahoma, this story reflects not only the Natchez tradition but also Cherokee and Creek influences. Before they were almost annihilated by the French in 1731, the Natchez lived in the lower Mississippi River area. Some of the Natchez who survived went to live with the Creeks in Alabama; others later joined the Cherokees and other tribes.

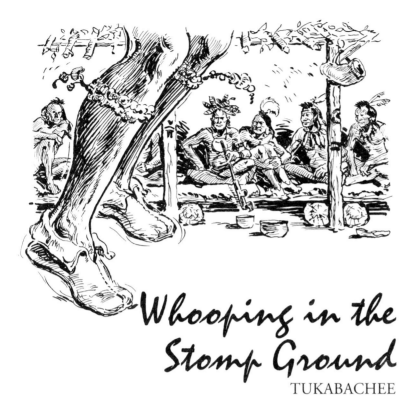

Whooping in the Stomp Ground

TUKABACHEE

In the beginning the Indians came pouring out of the earth like ants. Those who got out first looked back, saw crowds of other people coming, and said, "It will not be good. It must be stopped." And it stopped.

In those days they laid down the logs on the stomp ground. After they had arranged the logs and were seated on them, up came the tall Coweta and found them. Coweta said, "Who are you?"

"I am little Tukabachee." The Tukabachee chief held the *mikohoyanidja* (redroot medicine) in his right hand.

"What have you?"

"I have only the *miko hoyanidja* and my whoop."

"Let us hear you whoop," said Coweta.

"No."

"Yes, let us hear you whoop."

Tukabachee behaved very humbly and refused to whoop for

some time, but finally they agreed in order to please the strangers. Their leader arose, stomped on the ground, and whooped. The earth quivered as if there were an earthquake.

After the second whoop the Coweta leader said, "My friend, that will do." But having started, Tukabachee felt obliged to complete the four cries.

When he was through, the Coweta chief said, "We will be friends. Here is my medicine; let us combine the two."

So they united the *pasa* (button snakeroot) of the Coweta with the *miko hoyanidja* of the Tukabachee, and the combined medicine is the *sawatcka*.

After that, each tribe used both medicines.

The Tukabachees, a small but influential tribe, lived in a town on the Tallapoosa River near present-day Montgomery, Alabama. Tukabachee served as the capital of the Creek Nation. The friendship between the Tukabachees and the Cowetas did not last. They opposed each other in the Creek Indian War of 1813-14.

John Swanton, who recorded this story about the origin of Creek medicine, wrote: "The Tukabachee origin myth [was] related to me by Cook who had it from a Creek Indian known as Judge Nokosi. Judge Nokosi told him that it was fragmentary, and that the last person to know it in its completeness was an old man named Napoleon Yahola, who died before the Civil War."

The Animals' Revenge

CHEROKEE

In the old days the animals, birds, fishes, insects, and plants could talk, and they and the people lived together in peace and friendship. But as time went on the people increased so rapidly that their settlements spread over the whole earth, and the animals found themselves beginning to be cramped for room.

To make things worse, man invented bows, knives, blowguns, spears, and hooks, and with these weapons killed animals for food and for skins. The smaller creatures such as frogs and worms were crushed underfoot, out of pure carelessness or contempt. So the animals resolved to do something to insure their safety.

The bears were the first to meet in council in their townhouse under Kuwahi Mountain, the mulberry place. Old White Bear presided. After each in turn had complained of the way men killed their friends, ate their flesh, and used their skins for their own purposes, the animals decided to begin war at once.

"Let us make a bow and arrows and see if we can use against men the same weapon they use against us," a bear proposed.

So one bear got a nice piece of locust wood, and another sacrificed himself for the good of the rest by furnishing a piece of his intestines for the bowstring.

But when the bow and arrows were ready and the first bear stepped up to try them out, it was discovered that in letting the arrow fly after drawing back the bow, his long claws caught the string and spoiled the shot. Someone suggested they might trim his claws, which was done, and on a second try the arrow went straight to its mark. But the chief, old White Bear, objected. "We need long claws in order to climb trees," he said.

"One of us has already died to furnish the bowstring, and if we now cut off our claws we will all starve. It is better to keep the teeth and claws that nature gave us. It is clear that man's weapons are not intended for us."

The old chief dismissed the council, and the bears dispersed to the woods without having found a way to prevent the increase of the human race.

The deer next held a council under their chief, Little Deer.

"We will bring rheumatism to every hunter unless he asks pardon for killing one of our tribe," they said.

They sent a notice to the nearest settlement of Indians and told them what to do when necessity forced them to kill a member of the deer tribe. They must say a prayer and ask the deer's pardon.

"Whenever a deer is shot," the council told the hunters, "Little Deer, who is swift as the wind and cannot be wounded, runs swiftly to the spot. Bending over the bloodstains, he asks the deer if he heard the hunter pray for pardon. If the answer is yes, all is well, and Little Deer goes on his way.

"But if the reply is no, Little Deer follows the trail of the hunter, guided by the drops of blood on the ground. When he gets to the hunter's cabin, he enters invisibly and strikes the hunter with rheumatism, so that he becomes a helpless cripple."

The fishes and reptiles also had their complaints against human beings. They held a council together. "We will make our victims dream about snakes twining around them in slimy folds and blowing bad breath in their faces. We will make them dream of eating decayed fish, so they will lose their appetite, get sick, and die." This is why people dream about snakes and fish.

Finally, the birds, insects, and smaller animals came together for the same purpose.

The frog spoke first: "See how they have kicked me because I am ugly, they say, until my back is covered with sores." He showed the spots on his skin.

Then the bird—no one remembers now which one it was—condemned man "because he burns my feet off," referring to the way the hunter barbecues birds by impaling them on sticks over a fire, so their their feathers and feet are singed off.

Only the chipmunk ventured a good word for man. "He seldom hurts me, because I am so small." But his statement made the others so angry that they scratched the chipmunk with their claws. The stripes are on his back to this day.

Then they began to think up and name so many new diseases, one after another, that no one of the human race would have been able to survive.

When the plants, who were friendly to man, heard what the animals had done, they decided to defeat their evil designs. Each tree, shrub, and herb, down even to the grasses and moses, agreed to furnish a cure for a particular disease.

Each plant said, "I shall be ready to help man when he calls on me in his need."

That is how medicine came to man. The plants, every one of which has its use if we only knew it, furnish the remedies to counteract the diseases brought about by the vengeful animals. Even weeds were made for some good purpose, which we must find out for ourselves. When the medicine man does not know what medicine to use for a sick man, the spirit of the plant tells him.

"The Animals Revenge" highlights values in Indian life that we recognize today. First, the Indians learned not to abuse the natural world by wanton killing of animals, feeling nature could strike back as the animals do in the story. Today we too have learned we cannot exploit our natural resources indefinitely. Second, modern medicine recognizes that the Indians' use of herbal medicine may have been an intelligent approach to disease.

This story also illustrates the Indian belief that when illness or disaster struck, it was the work of vengeful spirits. Southern Indians turned to medicine men to set things right.

Medicine men had great influence in southern Indian life. Every town had at least one medicine man. Through incantations, rituals, and use of magic objects he could insure a good corn harvest, a successful hunt, a profitable raid. A Choctaw medicine man could put a spell on a ball player so that he would not be able to hit the goalpost, or he could charm the goalpost so that it could not be hit. An Alibamo medicine man could bring rain by feeding fish to a tie-snake in a river.

As healers, medicine men use a combination of herbal medicines and psychic powers. The main medicine of the Creeks was miko hoyanidja, made from the red willow root. It contained the same ingredient found today in aspirin. So the medicine man could conjure out the vengeful spirit causing illness at the same time he administered a pain-killing drug.

Medicine men were the keepers of tribal medicine bundles containing sacred objects handed down from ancient times. A sacred Cherokee object was the Ulunsuti, a flaming crystal from the head of the monster Uktema (p. 74). These sacred bundles carried by medicine men went west with the tribes when they were removed from the South.

Fire-in-the-Mouth

CHEROKEE

In the beginning of the world, when people and animals were all the same, there was only one tobacco plant. Everyone came to this plant for their tobacco until the Dagulku geese stole it and carried it far away to the south.

The people suffered without tobacco. One old woman grew so thin and weak that everyone said she would die unless she could get tobacco to keep her alive.

Various animals, first the large animals and then the smaller ones, volunteered to bring back the tobacco. But the Dagulku killed everyone before they could get to the plant. The little mole tried to reach the plant by burrowing underground, but the Dagulku saw his tunnel ridges and killed him as he emerged from the ground.

At last the hummingbird offered, even though the others said he was entirely too small and might as well stay home.

"Please let me try," he begged. So they showed him a plant in a field and told him, "Let us see how you would go about it."

In an instant the hummingbird was gone and they saw him perched on the plant, and then almost immediately he was back again. No one had seen him coming or going, because he was so swift.

"That is the way I'll do it," said the hummingbird.

They agreed to let him try.

The hummingbird flew away. When he came in sight of the tobacco, the Dagulku were guarding the plant carefully.

Quick as a flash the hummingbird darted down on the plant—tsa!—and snatched off the top with the leaves and seeds, and was off again before the Dagulku knew what had happened.

Before he reached home with the tobacco, the sick old woman had lost consciousness; her family thought she was dead. When the hummingbird arrived with the tobacco, he blew the smoke into her nostrils. With a cry of "Tsalu!" (fire in the mouth), the old woman opened her eyes and was well again.

For southern Indians, tobacco use was not a personal habit; it was reserved for special occasions. They believed tobacco had mystical powers. They smoked it to ward off evil spirits and to bring forth friendly ones. They smoked to put themselves in touch with the spirit world. They smoked as a gesture of friendliness, using the peace pipe. And they smoked before waging war.

The Creeks valued the tobacco plant so highly they made it a warrior and gave it the war name hitci. The Cherokees called tobacco tsalu, "fire in the mouth."

The tobacco cultivated by the southern Indians was not the tobacco of today, Nicotiana tabacum; it was Nicotiana rustica, native to the central Andes.

The Tobacco Warrior

CREEK

 A young man was courting a young woman. He told her he wanted to marry her and take her to his camp. She consented and they lay down together.

Later the man passed the spot where he and his wife had been and saw a pretty little plant growing there. He brushed the leaves from around it, and each time he passed that way he tended to the plant.

When the plant was about a foot high, the young man stripped off some of the leaves and smelled them. They smelled good to him. He threw some leaves in the fire, which made them smell even better.

He showed the leaves to the old men of his tribe, and told them how the plant had started.

The old men had noticed the plant, but they did not know what it was. Then one of them crumbled some of the leaves in his hand and put them in a hollowed-out corncob, lighted it, and smoked it. The smell was delightful.

"The leaves are good," the old men said.

This is how tobacco was given to human beings. Since the man and woman were happy and peacefully inclined to each other, tobacco has ever since been used in making peace among the Indian tribes.

3

Monsters, Heroes, and Spirits

In stories about monsters, heroes, and spirits we see reflected the southern Indians' beliefs about the three worlds: the Upper, the Under, and This World. In the Upper World everything was in perfect order and nothing unexpected could happen. Here lived the great spirits, Sun, Moon, Corn-mother, and departed souls. The Under World, where chaos reigned and anything could happen, was the home of monsters, witches, ghosts.

In This World human beings lived with plants and animals and an assortment of spirits, some friendly, some evil. Human beings were always trying to strike a balance between the perfect order of the Upper World and the chaos of the Under World.

One way they tried to establish order was to classify animals. Some animals, such as birds, they associated with the Upper World. To the Under World they assigned snakes, lizards, fish, and other creatures. Most four-footed animals were of This World; the deer was one of these.

But some animals gave the Indians trouble in their classification; these were the animals that seemed to belong to more than one group. They did not fit neatly into a classification. For example, the wildcat and mountain lion had many habits in common with other four-footed creatures, but they were nocturnal; they could see in the dark and came out at nightfall to hunt. The turtle was another four-footed animal who did not behave as most other four-footed animals; it spent a lot of time under water. The snake, which crawled on the ground, swam, and climbed trees, was probably the biggest problem of all.

Most of the monsters in Indian lore are these animals (or forms of them) that the Indians could not quite figure out. But some monsters, like Spear-finger, were like humans.

Monsters seemed to serve a purpose in Indian life, as they have done in many cultures: they provide a reason for tragedy and misfortune. If, for example, a man who was a good hunter had a long string of bad luck or suffered a disaster, his family would ascribe his troubles to a monster like the Lofa. When a child died, the Tlanuwa who swooped down and carried children away could be blamed.

Different from monsters were other spirit beings called ghosts or little people or forest people, among other names. These spirits played mischievous tricks on people, but they were not malicious. Often they helped people.

Then, too, sometimes a creature who was a monster in one story became a hero in another.

Finally, some stories tell of human beings who visited the Upper World in the sky or the watery Under World.

The Haunted Whirlpool
CHEROKEE

At the mouth of Suck Creek on the Tennessee River, about eight miles below Chattanooga, is a place the old-time Cherokees called Pot in the Water (or Boiling Pot). There dangerous whirlpools boiled up at intervals. Canoeists passing the spot hugged the bank, watchful for an eruption. They would pass only if the water was quiet.

Once two men approaching the water saw the water swirling ahead of them. "Quick," one of them said, "paddle for the bank."

They dug their paddles in the water and headed for shallow water, waiting for the whirlpool to subside. But to their horror the swirling waters came closer and closer in ever-widening circles.

"It is coming to get us," they shouted, grabbing for bushes along the bank.

Suddenly the canoe was caught in the vortex, and the men were thrown out and sucked under the water.

A huge fish seized one of the men, and he was never heard of again. The other man was flung around and around and down and down until he came to the bottom of the whirlpool. Then another swirling circle caught him and brought him up to the surface. He floated to shallow water and managed to crawl ashore.

Afterward the man told about his experience.

"When I was sucked down at the smallest circle of the whirlpool, the water seemed to open up below me. I could look down as through the roof beams of a house.

"On the bottom of the river I saw a great company of people. They looked up and beckoned to me to join them. As they raised their hands to grab me another whirl of water caught me and carried me up out of reach."

Aganunitsi's Search for the Magic Crystal

CHEROKEE

 In one of their battles with the Shawnees, the Cherokees captured the great medicine man, Aganunitsi [ah-gah-noo-nit-see].

Aganunitsi begged for his life. "If you will spare me," he said, "I will find for you the great wonder worker, the Ulunsuti [oo-lun-soo-tee]."

The Ulunsuti was a blazing crystal like a diamond star set in the forehead of the great Uktena serpent. The man who could possess the Ulunsuti would be able to do marvelous things. But everyone knew that capturing it was almost impossible, because meeting the Uktena meant certain death. The great serpent was as large around as a tree trunk, with horns on his head and scales glittering like sparks of fire. The Uktena could be wounded only in the seventh spot from the head, because under this spot was his heart.

The Cherokees warned Aganunitsi of the danger, but he only answered, "My medicine is strong and I am not afraid." So they sent him on his way to search for the Uktena.

The Uktena lay in wait in lonely places to surprise his victims. He especially haunted the dark passes of the Great Smoky Mountains. Aganunitsi knew this and went first to a gap in a mountain range on the north border of Cherokee country. Searching there, he found a monster blacksnake, larger than he had ever seen; but it was not what he was looking for.

Traveling south to the next mountain gap, he found a huge moccasin snake. This snake was not the right one, either, so Aganunitsi went on his way to the next gap, where he found a green snake. He called the people to see it, but they ran away in fear when they saw the immense snake coiled up in the path.

Coming to Bald Mountain, Aganunitsi found a great lizard basking in the sun; but, although it was large and terrible to look at, it was not what he wanted and he paid no attention to it. At another place he found a great frog squatting in the gap; when the people who came to look at it were frightened and ran away, he laughed at them for being afraid of a frog and went on to the next gap.

At the Gap of the Forked Antler and then at the enchanted Lake of Atagahi, he again found monstrous reptiles, but he said they were nothing. He believed the Uktena might be hiding in the deep water at a spot in Lake

Hiwassee, where other strange creatures had been seen. Arriving there, he dived in and swam far below the surface. He saw turtles and water snakes, and two immense sun perches rushed at him and retreated, but that was all. He tried other places as he kept moving southward. At last, on Gahuti Mountain, he found the Uktena asleep.

Turning noiselessly, Aganunitsi ran quickly down the mountainside as far as he could with one long breath. At the bottom of the slope he piled up a great circle of pine cones. Inside the circle he dug a deep trench. He set fire to the cones and climbed the mountain again.

He found Uktena still asleep. Putting an arrow to his bow, Aganunitsi shot the Uktena in the heart. The great snake raised his head, with the diamond in front flashing fire, and rushed at Aganunitsi. But Aganunitsi ran at full speed down the mountain, leaped over the circle of fire, and lay down on the ground inside.

The Uktena tried to follow, but the arrow had pierced his heart. In another moment he rolled over in a death struggle, spitting poison all over the mountainside. The poison drops could not penetrate the circle of fire, but only hissed and sputtered in the blaze. Aganunitsi was untouched except by one small drop which struck his head; but he did not know it.

The Uktena's blood, as poisonous as the froth, poured from the snake's wound and down the slope in a dark stream. It ran into the trench and left the man unharmed. The dying monster rolled over and over down the mountain, breaking down large trees in its path. When the Uktena's body was still, Aganunitsi called the birds in the woods to the feast; so many came that when they were through not even the bones were left.

After seven days, Aganunitsi returned by night to the spot. The body and the bones of the snake were gone, all eaten by the birds. But he saw a bright light shining in the darkness; going to it he found, resting on a low-hanging branch, where a raven had dropped it, the Ulunsuti crystal from the head of the

Uktena. He wrapped it up carefully and took it with him back to the Cherokee settlement. From that time he was the greatest medicine man in the tribe.

The people noticed a small snake hanging from Aganunitsi's forehead, where the single drop of poison from the Uktena had hit him. But as long as he lived, Aganunitsi himself never knew the snake was there.

Where the blood of the Uktena had filled the trench a lake formed. The water was black. In this water the women dyed the cane splits for their baskets.

The Uktena, the most fearsome of all monsters, was modeled after the snake. He actually had characteristics of three creatures: the body of a snake (associated with the Under World), the head of a deer (a creature of This World), and the wings of a bird (a creature of the Upper World).

This story is one of the most important in all Cherokee lore. It tells not only about the terrible Uktena but also explains the origin of the great magic crystal, the Ulunsuti. In the later 1800s, when Swimmer told this story to James Mooney, medicine men who possessed such crystals refused to show them to white men in case they would then lose their power.

The Uktena, the Indians believed, was originally a man, who after being changed into a snake was given the job of killing the sun, who was causing problems for man (see p.112). When the Uktena failed in this task he became jealous and resentful of human beings.

Other snake-like monsters in southern Indian lore included the olobit, the Natchez name for the sharp-breasted snake, meaning literally "walking terrapin." The Chickasaws had a monster called Nickin-fitcik (eye-star), who had a single eye in the middle of his forehead. If anything passed in front of his lair, the snake would catch it. The Koasatis told of a snake-crawfish with horns.

A Fight Between the Tlanuwa and the Uktena

CHEROKEE

The great hawk, the Tlanuwa [t'lah-noo-wah], nested on a steep cliff on the Little Tennessee River. Larger than any bird, the Tlanuwa could strike and kill a human with his sharp breastbone or pick him up and carry him off with his talons. He was always flying up and down the river to the settlements and carrying off dogs and children.

No one could reach the nest to kill the Tlanuwa, and when warriors tried to shoot him, the arrows only glanced off the bird.

At last the people went to a great medicine man for help. He made a long rope of bark, with loops in it for his feet, and had the people let him down from the top of the cliff when he knew the Tlanuwas were away from the nest.

When he had lowered himself on the rope just opposite the mouth of the cave, he realized he could not reach the cave because of the deep overhang. So he swung back and forth until he was near enough to pull himself into the cave with the hooked stick he carried.

On the cave floor he saw the bones of people and animals that had been brought there by the great hawks. In the nest he found four young Tlanwas; he pulled them out and threw them over the cliff into the deep water below. A great Uktena snake living in the river finished them off.

Just then the medicine man saw in the distance the two parent Tlanuwas returning, and he barely had time to climb back to the top of the cliff before they reached the nest. When they found the nest empty, the hawks were furious.

They circled round and round in the air until they saw the Uktena lift his head from the water. The Tlanuwas dived straight down, and while one seized the snake and flew with him far up in the sky, his mate attacked him and bit off piece after piece until nothing was left.

The Tlanuwas and the Uktena were so high in the sky that when the pieces of the snake fell they made holes in the rocks in the river.

Then the two Tlanuwas circled up and up until they went out of sight, and they have never been seen since.

This story could be called "A Battle Between Two Worlds," because here we see acted out the Indian belief about the enmity between the Upper World, represented by the Tlanuwa (hawk), and the Under World, represented by the Uktena snake. In many other Indian stories the hawk and the snake again are mortal enemies. The Tuscaroras, once the eastern neighbors of the Cherokees, told of a great rattlesnake which long ago lived by a creek and killed many Indians; at last a bald eagle killed it, and they were rid of a serpent that had devoured whole canoes full of Indians at a time.

The Cherokees located the Tlanuwa's nest in a real place—a cave halfway up a cliff on the north bank of the Little Tennessee River near the mouth of Citico Creek, Blount County, Tennessee. It was said that the holes made by the falling snake could still be seen at the placed called "Where the Tlanuwas cut it up," opposite the mouth of Citico Creek. On the other side of the river was the haunt of Spear-finger (p. 85). In recent years the construction of Tellico Dam destroyed this site, along with sites of at least twelve eighteenth-century Cherokee towns.

Two Cherokee storytellers, John Ax and Tagwadihi, told the story to James Mooney.

The Man-Eater and the Girl

CREEK

 A beautiful girl lived with her brothers on a riverbank. Her youngest brother was a Kuchehelochee [koo-che-he-lo-chee].

The mountain lion, Istepapa [iss-te-pa-pa], who is known to attack and eat human beings, approached their house on his boat and called to the girl.

"Come aboard," he said. The girl refused.

"I have some young lions on my boat. Please come and see them." The girl finally agreed.

Istepapa pushed his boat from shore and carried the girl away to his house. He put her in his wife's charge.

The next day, before starting off on a hunt, he said to the girl, "I like soup made of acorns and meat. Gather some acorns and wash them in the stream before I return."

When Istepapa had left, his wife said to the girl, "I am sorry he brought you here. He treats me cruelly and he will treat you the same way. When he fails to find any game, he eats a piece of my flesh with his acorns. He will punish you the same way. I will help you escape."

Istepapa's wife called Kotee, the water frog, from the stream. "Will you take the girl's place and wash the acorns?" Kotee said he would. Istepapa's wife instructed him, "When Istepapa asks you if the acorns have been washed, answer no."

Then she helped the girl climb over the house, urging her to run as fast as possible to her brothers' house.

When Istepapa returned, he called out to the girl, "Have you washed my acorns?" He heard a voice answer, "No."

Again Istepapa asked, "Have you washed my acorns?" Again the hidden voice, Kotee's, replied, "No."

Mystified, Istepapa went down to the water where the voice had come from. Kotee heard him coming and jumped into the stream. Istepapa plunged in, too, thinking the girl had made the splash.

"Little girl, why do you run away from me?" he called out gently.

Getting no results, Istepapa returned to his house and found his wheel, which could find anything that was lost. Istepapa threw the wheel away from him; it ran a short distance and returned. Istepapa tried throwing it in several directions, but each time it came back.

At last he threw the wheel down in his yard. It immediately went over the house and began following the girl's trail. Istepapa followed it.

Moving fast, they soon caught sight of the little girl, who was singing as she ran:

"I wonder if I can reach my brothers' house before they catch me.

I wonder if I can reach my brothers' house before they catch me."

Meanwhile, the girl's brother Kuchehelochee, playing in the woods, thought he heard his sister's voice in the distance. he said to his brothers, "I think I hear our sister calling."

The girl kept running, chased by Istepapa and the wheel, and singing:

"I wonder if I can reach my brothers' house before they catch me.

I wonder if I can reach my brothers' house before they catch me."

Kuchehelochee was now convinced that it was his sister's voice he heard. He called his brothers and this time they too heard her singing. They said to Kuchehelochee, "Stay here. You are too young to help."

But Kuchehelochee insisted on going with them. They saw

their sister and the wheel and Istepapa close behind her. As they got closer, the brothers shot arrows at the wheel but could not stop it.

Their sister passed them and ran into the house. The wheel followed, but Kuchehelochee struck it with the little wooden paddle he used in parching his food, and the wheel rolled to one side of stopped.

Istepapa still came on. The brothers shot at him but could not stop him. Then Kuchehelochee struck the lion on the head with his wooden paddle and killed him.

"You are the bravest of all," his brothers told Kuchehelochee. "You have saved our sister's life."

The mountain lion, also called the panther and the cougar, at one time flourished in the south, but civilization pushed him west. A few of these animals, called Florida panthers, survive in Florida

William O. Tuggle, who collected Creek stories, recorded the story about 1880.

Captured by a Lofa
CHICKASAW

A group of Chickasaw men belonging to the Wildcat clan went hunting a long way from home. After making camp they scattered to see what they could find, but remained within call of one another. They had agreed that if anyone encountered trouble he would shout for help.

One man ventured farther than he realized. He was tired and sat down to rest. He had not been sitting long when he heard what sounded like a large creature crashing through the woods. Sure enough, through the trees he saw approaching him a huge

Lofa, ten feet tall. The Lofa looked something like a man, but he had long arms and a small head.

The Lofa said to the hunter, "What are you doing here? You are intruding my land. You'd better get up and go home."

The hunter decided he had no choice but to act as if he were not afraid, so he sat still without speaking.

The Lofa continued, "If you do not get up and go away I will tie you up and carry you to my place."

"Do so if you can," retorted the man. And the Lofa grabbed him. At first if seemed that the hunter might have a chance to win as he struggled with the Lofa; he was even able to throw the huge creature to the ground. But the Lofa smelled so bad that the hunter weakened. The Lofa overpowered him, hung him up in a tree, and went away.

The hunter hung there all night. When he did not appear at camp, the other hunters began searching for him. They found him and cut the grapevine by which he was fastened, and he fell to the ground.

"What happened to you? Who did this to you?" they asked. But the hunter would say nothing. The others decided he had seen a ghost. Eventually, though, he was able to talk and tell what had happened.

After that, although he loved hunting, he would never go out unless someone was with him.

Spear-finger

CHEROKEE

Long, long ago there lived in the mountains a terrible witch whose food was human livers. She could take on any shape she liked, but in her usual form she looked much like a woman. Her body was covered with skin hard as rock, and on her right hand she had a long, stony forefinger of bone, like an awl or spearhead, with which she could stab anyone to whom she could get near enough. She was called Utlunta, or Spear-finger.

She traveled all over the mountains around the heads of streams and in the dark passes of Nantahala, always hungry and always looking for victims. A favorite haunt was the gap on the trail where Chilhowee Mountain comes down to the river.

Sometimes the woman would approach children along the trail near the village where they were playing or picking strawberries. She would coax them, "Come, my children, come to your granny and let me dress your hair."

When a little girl laid her head on the woman's lap to be petted and combed, Spear-finger gently ran her fingers through the child's hair until she went to sleep. Then she stabbed the child through the heart or the back of the neck with her long awl finger which she had kept hidden under her robe. She took out the child's liver and ate it.

Spear-finger entered a house by taking the appearance of one of the family who had gone out for a short time. She watched for a chance to stab someone with her long finger and take out the liver. She could stab a person without being noticed, and often even the victim did not know it at the time—for it left no wound and caused no pain—but went about his own affairs, until he began to feel weak and gradually pined away. He was sure to die, because Spear-finger had taken his liver.

When the Cherokees went out in the fall to burn the leaves to get the chestnuts on the ground, according to their custom, they were never safe. Spear-finger was always on the lookout. As soon as she saw the smoke rise, she knew Indians were there and sneaked up to try to surprise one alone. So the people tried to stay together and were cautious about allowing a stranger to approach. If one of them went down to the spring for a drink, the others never knew but it might be the liver-eater that came back and sat with them.

Sometimes she looked like a witch. Once or twice, when far out from the Cherokee settlements, a solitary hunter had seen a woman with a queer-looking hand going through the woods singing to herself:

Liver, I eat it. Su-su-sai.

Liver, I eat it. Su-su-sai.

The song chilled the hunter's blood. He knew he had seen the liver-eater, and he hurried away before she could see him.

At last a great council was held to devise some way to get rid of Spear-finger. The people came from all around. After much talk they decided to trap her in a pit where all the warriors could attack her. So they dug a deep hole across the trail and covered it with earth and grass as if the ground had never been disturbed. Then they lighted a large fire of brush near the trail and hid in the laurel bushes. They knew Spear-finger would come as soon as she saw the smoke.

Sure enough, they soon saw a woman coming along the trail. She looked like an old woman they knew in the village. She walked slowly, with one hand under her blanket. When she stepped on the pit-covering she tumbled into the deep hole. Immediately she showed her true nature. Instead of the feeble old woman, she was the terrible Spear-finger, with her stony skin and her sharp awl finger flashing out in every direction trying to stab someone.

The warriors rushed out to surround the pit. They shot their arrows at the witch, but the arrows bounced off her stony skin and fell useless in the pit. Spear-finger tried to climb out of the pit to get at the warriors, but they kept out of her way.

They were only wasting their arrows. Then a bird, the titmouse, began to sing from a tree overhead. The warriors thought he was singing *unahu* (heart), meaning they should aim at the witch's heart. They shot their arrows where the heart should be, but the arrows only glanced off with the flint heads broken.

The warriors kept up the fight with the witch without result until another bird, little Tsikilili, the chickadee, flew down from a tree and alighted on the witch's right hand. The men took this as a sign they must aim there. They were right, for Spear-finger's heart was on the inside of her hand, which she kept doubled in a fist—the awl hand with which she had stabbed so many people.

Now Spear-finger was frightened. She began to rush furiously at her attackers with her long finger and to jump about to dodge the arrows. At last a lucky arrow struck just where the awl joined her wrist, and she fell dead.

Ever since, Tsikilili, the chickadee, is known as a truth teller. When a man is away on a journey, if this bird comes and perches near the house and chirps his song, the man's family and friends know he will soon be safely home.

Another human monster in Cherokee stories is Nun-yun-uwi, the Stone Man. Some say there was a pair of monsters, husband and wife.

The Creeks had a parallel in Big Rock Man, who was finally killed when the people took Rabbit's advice to shoot him in the ear.

Near Lake Okeechobee in Florida, the Seminoles said, were giant men, tall as trees, who had the power to cause human illness. People who had the sickness talked about seeing giants.

Besides the Lofa (p.83), the Chickasaws feared the Tiboli, a man-like creature with a club-shaped arm, who sometimes was seen or heard pounding on trees.

The Long Evil Being looked like a man but had a shriveled face; long, pointed ears; and a long nose. In Choctaw lore this creature lived in dense woods near swamps, where he would confront lonely hunters far from home.

The Cave of the Thunder People

CHEROKEE

In old times the Cherokees danced often, sometimes all night. Once, at a dance at Sakwiyi, at the head of the Chattahoochee River, two young women with beautiful long hair came in. No one knew who they were or where they had come from. They danced with several young men, and in the morning slipped away before anyone knew they were gone.

A young warrior had fallen in love with one of the sisters and had already asked her (as the Cherokee custom was, through an old man) to marry him. The young woman had replied that her brother at home must first be consulted; she promised to return with an answer at the next dance a week later. In the meantime, she said, "If you really love me you must prove it by fasting until I return." The eager young man agreed.

On the night of the next dance the young warrior was on hand early. He had impatiently been counting the days until he would see the young woman again. Late in the evening the two sisters appeared suddenly, as they had before.

"Our brother is willing," they told the young warrior. "After the dance we will take you to our home. But we must warn you, if you tell anyone where you are going or what you see, you will die."

The young man danced with the sisters again, and about dawn the three left in order to avoid being followed. The women led the way along a trail through the woods, until they came to a creek. Without hesitating, the two women stepped into the water. Surprised, the young man paused on the bank and thought to himself, "They are walking in the water; I can't do that."

The Chickasaws had a different explanation of thunder. When it thunders, they said, the Great Chief of Thunder (Ishto Eloha Alkaiasto) is angry. And when it rains and blows hard, the Holy People above are at war above the clouds.

As if he had spoken, the women knew what he had been thinking. "This is not water," they said, "this is the road to our house." He hesitated but they urged him on until he stepped into the water and discovered it was only soft grass.

The trail soon reached a large stream which the young man recognized as the Tallulah River. Again the women plunged boldly in, and again the warrior hesitated on the bank, thinking, "That water is deep; I will drown if I go in."

But the women assured him, "This is not water, but the main trail that goes past our house, which is now close by." When he stepped in, instead of water he found tall waving grass.

Soon they reached a cave under Tallulah Falls. The women entered, but the warrior hesitated. "This is our house," they called to him.

"Come in. Our brother will soon be home." The warrior heard low thunder from a distance. He stepped inside the cave and watched in amazement as the women took off their long hair and hung it up on a rock. Their heads were smooth as pumpkins. "Their hair is not hair at all," he thought.

The woman he had fallen in love with invited him to come and sit beside her. When he looked at the seat, he realized it was a large turtle, which reared up and stretched out its claws as if angry at being disturbed. "That's a turtle. I can't sit down on it," the young man said. But the woman insisted it was a seat.

Another, louder roll of thunder sounded through the cave, and the woman said, "Our brother is nearly home."

Suddenly there was a great thunder clap just behind the warrior. Turning quickly, he saw a man standing in the cave's doorway.

"This is my brother," said the woman. He came in and sat down on the turtle, which again reared up and stretched out his claws.

The brothers said to the warrior, "I am about to start out to a council meeting. I would like you to go with me."

"I will go with you," said the warrior, "if you will let me have a horse." The young woman went out and came back leading a great Uktena snake, that curled and twisted along the whole length of the cave.

The warrior was frightened. "That is a snake," he said. "I can't ride that." But the others insisted it was a riding horse. The brother said to the woman, "He may like it better if you bring him a saddle, and bracelets for his arms." She went out again and brought a saddle and armbands; but the saddle was another turtle, which they fastened on the Uktena's back, and the bracelets were living, slimy snakes, which they prepared to twist around the warrior's wrists

Pale with fear, the warrior said, "What kind of horrible place is this? I could never live with snakes and creeping things."

"You are a coward," the brother said angrily. Then lightning flashed from his eyes and struck the warrior, and a terrible crash of thunder stretched him senseless on the ground.

When at last he came to himself, he was standing in the water and both his hands grasped a laurel bush that grew out from the bank. There was no trace of the cave or the Thunder People. He was alone in the forest.

Making his way out, he finally reached his settlement. He had been gone so long that his people thought him dead. His friends questioned him closely about what had happened to him. Forgetting the warning of the young women, he told the story. But in seven days he died, for no one can come back from the Under World and tell about it and live.

Escape from a Cliff Cave
CHEROKEE

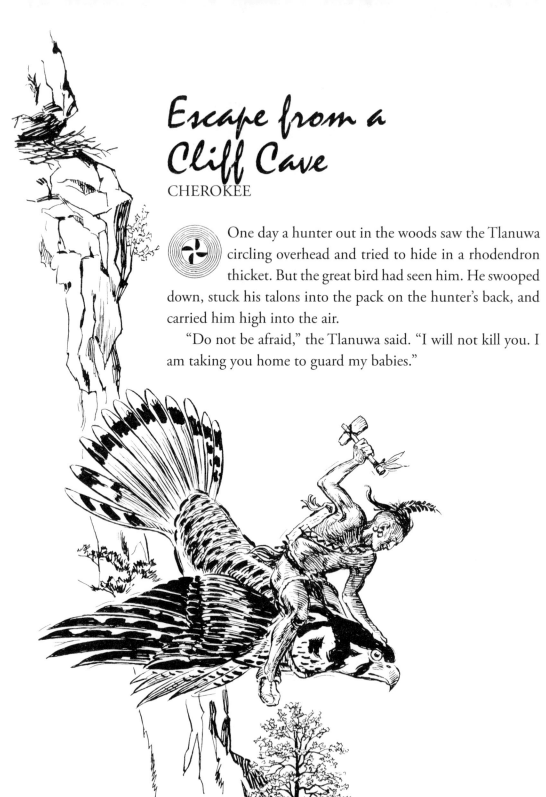

One day a hunter out in the woods saw the Tlanuwa circling overhead and tried to hide in a rhododendron thicket. But the great bird had seen him. He swooped down, stuck his talons into the pack on the hunter's back, and carried him high into the air.

"Do not be afraid," the Tlanuwa said. "I will not kill you. I am taking you home to guard my babies."

Soon the hawk landed on a rock ledge at the mouth of a cave high on a cliff. She set the hunter down and flew away.

The hunter peered into the dark cave and saw a nest of sticks with two baby hawks in it. They opened their mouths and cawed as he approached.

"I am not your mother," he said angrily. "She has left me here to guard you, and I have no way to escape."

After a time the mother hawk returned with a freshly killed deer. She tore it into pieces and gave the first piece to the man. Then she fed her babies.

For many days the hunter stayed in the cave. Each morning the mother hawk flew away and each evening she returned with a deer or a bear. Always she fed the hunter before she fed the babies.

The hunter watched as the baby hawks grew bigger and bigger. They began to stretch their wings and flap around on the cave floor.

"Take me back to my people," the hunter begged as the Tlanuwa returned one evening. "You do not need me to guard your babies. They are big birds now." But the Tlanuwa ignored the hunter.

The young hawks grew larger than the hunter. As he watched them practicing flying in the cave, he thought of a way to escape. He took a strap from his hunting pack and tied it to his leg. He found his stone ax still in his pack. When the mother Tlanuwa had left for the day's hunting, he spoke to the larger of the young birds.

"We will learn to fly together. Come to the ledge and I will show you what to do."

The young bird trusted the hunter and did as he was told.

"First," said the hunter, "I will strap myself on your back." The young bird, eager to soar off the cliff, let the hunter climb onto his back.

"Now, push off," the hunter cried. And the young bird and

the man soared off into the air.

As the bird flapped his wings to fly higher, the man reached for his ax and struck the bird on the head. The dazed bird started to fall slowly to earth. Air from below held up his wings, so it was almost as if he were flying. The bird revived and tried to fly up to the nest.

But the hunter struck him again, and the bird slowly floated down, landing in the top of a tall poplar tree.

As the bird came to his senses, the hunter untied the strap holding him to the young Tlanuwa. And just as the bird lifted off to fly away, the man plucked a feather from his wing.

The hunter climbed down the tree and returned to his home. When he looked in his pack for the feather, he found a stone instead.

Riding a Monster Turtle

CREEK

 One summer seven men set out on a hunting expedition. In the heat they became thirsty and began longing for water.

When they encountered a monster bull turtle, they said to one another, "He surely will go toward water. Let's follow him."

One of the hunters said, "Let us get on his back." He and five other men climbed on the turtle's back. But the seventh man would not. "It might not be good to do so," he said, and walked along behind.

Soon they sighted a big lake. When the turtle reached the shore the men on his back tried to get off, but they found they had stuck to the turtle. So they stayed on the monster's back and were carried into the lake.

The man on foot watched the turtle and the six men until they reached the middle of the lake, where they disappeared, leaving numerous bubbles. The seventh man stood looking at the lake for some time and then returned home.

When he reported what had happened, the relatives of the six men quickly assembled on the square ground. They sang, accompanied by a kettle drum and a gourd rattle, and then made one step in the direction of the lake.

They did the same thing the next night and made another step toward the lake. In this way they approached the lake a step at a time until they reached it. On the edge of the water they continued their song.

Finally they heard a disturbance from the middle of the lake. A snake approached them and laid his head humbly on the ground in front of them.

"You are not the one we want," they told him, and the snake went back into the lake.

The people continued singing, and soon another snake came out of the lake. "You are not the one, either," they said, and he went back. A third snake came, but they sent him back too.

Finally, with a great swashing of water, the monster turtle emerged from the water. He laid his head humbly on the ground before the people.

"What shall we do with him?" the people said. "He must be good for something."

They cut the turtle up into small pieces, leaving only the shell. Part of the turtle's body they took to use as medicine.

They all returned to their town rejoicing. "The medicine we got from the turtle we will use with the song of the waters as our revenge," they said.

The Hero Panther

CREEK

A man and his wife went with their dogs on a bear-hunting trip.

One day the man followed his dogs to a rough, rocky place on the water's edge. The dogs barked and yelped and the man supposed they had found a bear. He saw something dash out from the rocks, seize one of his dogs, and carry it back.

It was a huge lizard.

The man turned and ran back toward his camp. About halfway he realized the lizard was close behind him. The man dropped to the ground and lay flat on his chest, but the lizard picked him up in his mouth and started carrying him back to his den.

The man looked from time to time to see how close they were to the rocks. He knew that in a minute the lizard was going to cut him in pieces and eat him. But suddenly he heard a scratching noise in a tree near by. The lizard heard it too and dropped the man.

The noise had been made by a panther, who jumped down on the lizard, scratching him badly, and chased him back to his den.

The man dared not move, expecting the panther to attack him when he returned. In a short time the panther was back. He said to the man, "Are you dead?"

At first the man did not answer. Again the panther spoke: "You are not going to die, for I will protect you."

"No, I am not dead," said the man.

"Well, get up," said the panther. The panther licked him all over and said, "Can you stand up?"

Seeing that he could not, the panther made him climb on his back. The man protested, but the panther said, "Oh, I can carry you. Sometimes I carry two deer, and I can carry you just as easily."

The panther or mountain lion was a monster in an earlier story. Here he is the hero-rescuer, a friend to man.

On the way back to the man's camp they came first upon the shot pouch and then the gun which the man had dropped when being chased by the monster lizard. The panther told him to pick them up and carry them.

Reaching a point near the camp, the panther set the man down and told him to go the rest of the way himself. The man invited him to come to his camp and get all the food he wanted, but the panther refused.

Before leaving the hunter, though, he said, "My friend, I have two nephews whom you must never harm."

"Who are they?"

"One is Wildcat and the other is Housecat. They are of my species. Never kill any of my species."

The next summer the man was again out hunting and heard turkeys gobbling. He discovered one of them high in a pine tree and was preparing to shoot it when he noticed a wildcat crawling up the tree toward it. The hunter stopped and watched. When the wildcat leaped at the turkey, it missed and fell to the ground with a painful cry.

Remembering what the panther had done for him, the man ran to help the wildcat. He found that he had lost one of his eyes in the fall. "Have you hurt yourself?" the man said.

When the wildcat heard the man speak, he pulled out his other eye and then ran away.

The Hunter and His Dog

CHICKASAW

One winter a man of the Red Skunk people went off hunting with his dog and made camp near a mountain. After several days he had killed lots of deer and bear, and he began to think of returning home.

On the very morning he was to begin his journey home, the mountain began to smoke. He set off, but after a time he saw that he was back in the same spot where he had camped at the foot of the mountain. For several days he tried desperately to get home, but he always ended up where he had started.

Finally he decided to stop and sleep. As he was dozing, he looked up to see a strange creature, about the size of a man, approaching him. The creature said nothing to the hunter and eventually went away.

The hunter's dog said, "You cannot stay here all night. If you do you will surely die."

"What shall I do?" the man said.

"If you want to escape," said the dog, "when the creature comes back, shoot an arrow as far as you can. The creature will chase the arrow. Then begin running for home, and get ready to shoot another arrow if he catches up with you again."

Soon the creature appeared again, and the hunter shot an arrow far away. While the creature ran after it, he and his dog ran in the other direction.

When the creature found the arrow, he turned around and followed the man and his dog. As he got close, the man shot off another arrow. This continued until the hunter ran out of arrows and the creature was close behind. "Quick," the dog said, "let's get in this hollow tree."

They crawled in, and the dog licked at the opening until he had licked it closed. The creature could not get to them in the tree and finally left. The next morning the dog licked again at the hole until it was open.

Free of the creature at last, the man and his dog made their way home.

The Sky Canoes
ALIBAMO

Once some people from the Upper World decided to come down to earth to have a ball game. They descended in canoes, singing and laughing, and played ball on a little prairie. When they had finished playing they got back into their canoes, rose into the sky, and disappeared.

They liked the spot where they had chosen to play and came back to it often, always laughing and singing.

A man had seen the canoes coming down. He hid in some bushes and watched as the Upper World people played ball.

The ball got away from the players and rolled close to where the man was hiding. A woman ran after it, and as she reached to pick it up, the man caught her. The other people got into the canoes and disappeared into the sky.

The man married the woman and they had several children.

One day the children said, "Father, we want fresh meat. Go and hunt deer for us." After he had brought meat home, the mother said, "Tell your father to go again, farther away this time, and bring back more deer."

After the man had set off, the woman put the children into a canoe and they started up to the sky, singing. The man heard them and ran back. He pulled the canoe down to the ground.

The woman now made a small canoe. The next time her husband went hunting, she put the children in the small canoe and got in the other one. They started up. But her husband came back in time to pull the children down. The mother disappeared into the sky.

The children missed their mother. So the man and the children got into the small canoe and set off to find her.

Soon they came to an old woman's house. The man said, "We have come because the children want to see their mother."

The old woman said, "Their mother is dancing over at that house." She cooked squash for her visitors. The children thought, "It is too little for us," but when they ate one squash, another appeared in its place. Then the old woman broke a corncob into pieces and gave them to the family.

They set out to the house where the mother was dancing. When they saw her they threw a piece of corncob at her, but it missed her. She danced right through her children and her husband.

They threw another corncob at her and it also missed her. But she said, "I smell something." When they threw a corncob again, it hit her. She said, "My children have come," and she ran up to them. They all got into the canoe and returned to This World.

Later, when the father was hunting, the mother and the children went up again into the sky. When he returned, the father got in a canoe, sang, and started up into the sky to join his family.

But he looked down at the ground. He fell back and was killed.

The King of the Tie-Snakes

CREEK

 A chief sent his son with a message to another chief, entrusting the boy with a treasured bowl which he would carry as a symbol of his father's authority.

Along the way the son stopped to play with some boys who were throwing stones into a stream. Without thinking, he threw his bowl into the water, and it sank. He was afraid to go to the neighboring chief without the bowl, and he did not want to return home to tell his father what he had done.

He jumped into the stream and, swimming to the spot where the bowl had sunk, he dived down. Deeper and deeper he went. It was dark under the surface, and he could barely see. As he probed around for the bowl, he felt himself seized by slimy creatures. The tie-snakes carried him to an underwater cave.

Peering into the cave's murkiness, the boy saw the king of the tie-snakes seated on a platform. "Climb the platform," his captors ordered.

As he slowly walked toward the platform and lifted a foot to step up on it, the boy saw it was a mass of tie-snakes. It was impossible to get a foothold on the writhing mass. He kept trying, and the tie-snakes kept urging him to climb it.

Finally he succeeded in getting up on the platform, and the king motioned him to sit beside him.

"See that feather?" said the king, pointing to a long, handsome feather in the corner of the cave. "You can have it." The boy moved toward the feather to take it, but the feather slid out of his grasp. Three times he tried, and only on the fourth attempt was he able to hold it.

"That tomahawk also is yours," said the king.

But as the boy reached out to take it, the tomahawk glided away. After four attempts, the boy grasped it.

Then the king said, "You may return to your father after three days. When he asks where you have been, you must answer, 'I know what I know.' But on no account tell him what you do know.

"When your father needs my help," the king continued, "walk toward the east and bow three times to the rising sun, and I will be there to help him."

After three days the tie-snakes took the boy to the spot where he had dived in and placed the bowl in his hands. The boy swam to the bank and ran back to his father, who was overjoyed to see him. The boy told about the tie-snake king and his offer to help. Not long afterward, the chief was warned of an attack by his enemies.

"Go and ask the tie-snake king for help," he said to his son.

The son took the feather and the tomahawk he had been given in the cave and went toward the east and bowed three times to the rising sun.

The king of the tie-snakes stood before him. "What do you wish?" he said.

"My father needs your help."

"Go and tell him not to fear. His enemies will attack, but your people will not be harmed. Tomorrow everything will be all right."

The boy raced back to his father with the message.

The enemy approached the chief's town and launched an attack. But no one was harmed. The chief, his warriors, and the entire town rested well that night.

In the morning they looked outside the town and saw their attackers all held tightly by the tie-snakes. The chief's men captured the enemy, and the chief made peace with his foes.

Spirit Folk

Spirit folk in southern Indian lore usually lived in forests. Most were friendly toward humans, but they were often mischievous. In other cultures these creatures were called fairies, dwarf leprechauns, sprites, goblins, elves.

BOHPULI *Choctaw*

These were friendly little peop about two feet tall who threw sticks an stones at people to tease them. Myster ous noises in the woods, it was believe came from the Bohpuli [bo-poo-lee They helped the medicine men, wh consulted with them.

KASHIKANCHAK *Choctaw*

This female goblin liked to ste children. She carried a large bag to p them in. Choctaw mothers threatene children who misbehaved by sayin "Kashikanchak [kah-shih-kan-chak] w come and get you."

NUNNEHI *Cherokee*

The Nunnehi [noo-nuh-hee] we invisible except when they wanted to seen, and then they looked just like oth Indians. Always friendly, they help the lost or injured, returning them their homes. More than once they se their own warriors to save the Cheroke from defeat in war. They lived in Georg and North Carolina mountains in tov houses, especially on bald mountai such as Pilot Knob.

NUNWI TSUNDI *Cherokee*

Known as the Little People, these handsome spirits were helpful and kind, especially adept at finding lost children and returning them to their parents. To help people they sometimes worked at night clearing fields or gathering corn. People could hear them talking as they worked, but if they went out to watch the Little People, they would die.

YAGANASHA *Chickasaw*

These friendly little people carried human beings off to make them medicine men. [ee-yah-gah-nah-shah]

DETSATA *Cherokee*

This little fellow spent all his time hunting birds with a blowgun. As a boy he ran away to the woods to avoid a scratching. Mischievously he sometimes hid an arrow from a bird hunter. When the hunter would fail to find his arrow, he would say, "Detsata [det-sah-tah], you have my arrow. If you don't give it to me, I will scratch you." When he would look again, he would find the arrow. [Scratching the skin was thought to release the evil spirit that was causing the person to misbehave.]

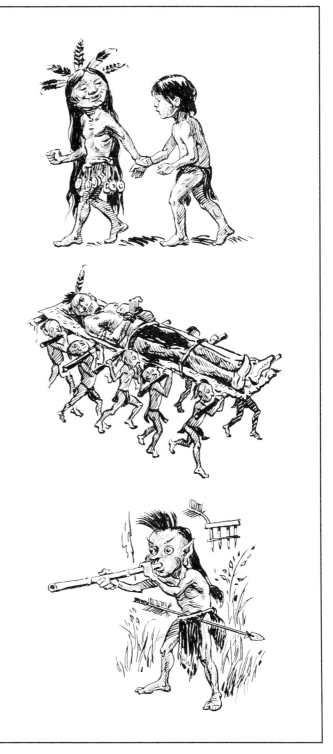

4

Sun, Moon, and Stars

In Indian stories the sun, moon, and stars are alive and have feelings just as human beings do.

To the Cherokees the sun was a woman, and the moon was her brother. To the Creeks and Choctaws the sun was a male. To all the tribes, however, the sun was recognized as the source of light and warmth, the source of life itself. The Choctaws believed the sun watched them with its great blazing eye; and if it did not, they were doomed. The motif of the open hand with the eye in the center appears in many ceremonial artifacts of the southern Indians.

Brothers Who Followed the Sun

CHOCTAW

Long, long ago two young brothers, Tashka and Walo, decided they wanted to follow Sun. Every morning they saw him come up over the edge of the earth, pass high overhead, and late in the day die in the west.

So they waited until Sun was directly overhead and then set out after him. At first they walked at an easy pace, but in a while Tashka said to Walo, "Sun is too far ahead of us. We must walk faster."

The brothers picked up their pace, but Sun stayed ahead of them.

"We must run or we will never catch him," Tashka urged his brother.

They started to run, but that night when Sun died, the brothers were still in their own country.

"We will catch him tomorrow," they vowed.

That night they slept, and the next day when Sun was again overhead they set off once more to follow him. The brothers continued pursuing Sun until they had grown to be young men. At last they reached a great body of water. The only land was the shore on which they stood.

They saw Sun die, sinking into the water. They passed over the water and entered Sun's house with him. Sun's house was the great dome of the sky.

All around the brothers were stars and Moon. Moon was a woman, Sun's wife. Moon said to the brothers, "How have you come here, so far from home?"

"We have followed Sun on his daily journey since we were boys."

Then Sun said, "Why have you followed me? It is not time for you to come here."

"We wanted to see where you went when you died," the brothers answered.

Sun spoke to his wife: "Boil water and bring it to me in a pot." Sun put the young men in the boiling water and rubbed

Retold from an account by a Choctaw of Bayou Lacomb, Louisiana, to David I. Bushnell, Jr.

them until their skin came off.

Sun then said, "I will return you to your home. But you must not speak a word to anyone for four days. If you speak during that time you will die. If you do not speak, you will live and prosper.

"Do you know the way home?" Sun continued.

"No," replied the brothers.

So Sun took them to the edge of the sky, where they looked down to earth. "I do not see our home," Tashka said.

"I cannot see it, either," Walo said.

Sun called a large buzzard and placed the brothers on his back. Buzzard started toward earth. The brothers had no trouble keeping their hold on the bird's back until they passed into clouds. A strong wind was blowing and Buzzard was blown about; the brothers hung on desperately.

But they reached earth safely. Buzzard put them down in the trees near their home.

The brothers were resting under the trees, recovering from their frightening journey, when an old man passed by and recognized them. He did not speak to them, however, but continued down the road until he met the brothers' mother. "Your boys have come back," he said. "But they are men now."

The mother ran toward Tashka and Walo. She wanted to know where they had been and what had happened to them. At first they did not answer, because of what Sun had said would happen if they spoke.

But their mother insisted, "You must tell me where you have been." So Tashka and Walo told her about their long journey to the end of the earth and what Sun had said about not talking for four days.

The mother worried because she had forced her sons to speak. But she took them to her house, and all the neighbors came in. The brothers told everything they had seen and done during their years of following Sun.

When they had told everything, they died and went up into the great sky to remain forever.

Buzzard and Wren Rescue the Sun

ALIBAMO

 An old woman put the sun into an earthen pot and kept it there. Rabbit wanted the sun and stayed at her house, hoping to get it.

He said to the people assembled there, "Sing for me so I can dance."

"We don't know how to sing for you," they answered.

"Sing, 'Rabbit, Rabbit, Rabbit,'" he said.

So they sang, and he danced.

While he was dancing he said, "Move the pot toward me." And they moved it toward him.

"I am dancing like a crazy person," said Rabbit. "Move the pot closer."

When they moved it closer, he seized the pot and ran away.

As he ran, Rabbit kept hitting the pot against the bushes. When he hit the pot against a hornbeam tree, it broke in pieces, and the sun fell out.

Then all the creatures assembled to plan how they could set the sun up in the sky. The flying things tried to move the sun, but they failed. Then Wren tried, and the sun rose a short distance and fell back again.

Wren said, "If someone would help me I could carry it up."

Buzzard said, "I will help." So Buzzard and Wren worked together; grasping the sun on each side, they flew up with it and placed it in the sky.

When Buzzard and Wren came back, the people said to Buzzard, "You shall eat animals that have died."

To Wren they said, "You shall wash in cold water every morning and you will never be sick."

When an eclipse of the sun or moon started, the Creeks, Seminoles, and Cherokees believed a great toad was swallowing the sun or moon. The people ran about beating drums and shooting arrows to frighten the toad away.

The buzzard was held in high esteem by the southern Indians. They believed that because he ate carrion he was immune to disease, so they placed a buzzard feather over a door or in a medicine bundle to ward off disease.

The Daughter of the Sun

CHEROKEE

The sun lived on the other side of the sky vault, but her daughter lived in the middle of the sky, directly above the earth. Every day as the sun climbed the sky arch she stopped at her daughter's house for lunch.

The sun hated people on earth because they could not look at her without screwing up their faces. She said to her brother the moon, "My grandchildren are ugly; they grin all over their faces when they look at me." But the moon said, "I think they are very handsome. They always smile when they see me in the sky at night." The moon's rays were mild.

The sun was jealous and planned to kill all the people. Every day when she got near her daughter's house she sent down such sultry rays that there was a great fever.

People died by the hundreds, and there was fear that no one would be left. The people went for help to the Little Men.

"The only way to save yourselves," said the Little Men, "is to kill the sun."

The Little Men made medicine and changed two men to snakes, the spreading-adder and the copperhead. They sent the snakes to watch near the door of the daughter of the sun and to bite the sun when she came next day.

The two snakes hid near the house until the sun came. When the spreading-adder was about to spring, the sun's bright light blinded him. He could only spit out yellow slime, as he does to this day when he tries to bite. The sun called him a nasty thing and went into the house. The copperhead crawled off without trying to do anything.

So the people still died from the heat. They went a second time to the Little Men. "Please help us," they said.

The Little Men made medicine again and changed one man into the great Uktena and another into the rattlesnake. Then they sent them to watch near the house and kill the sun when she came to eat.

The Little Men made the Uktena very large, with horns, and everyone thought he could surely do the work. But the rattlesnake was so quick and eager that he coiled up just outside the house, and when the sun's daughter opened the door to look out for her mother, he sprang up and bit her and she fell dead in the doorway. The rattlesnake was so upset at his mistake that he forgot to wait for the sun, but went back to the people. And the Uktena was so angry about what had happened that he went back, too.

When the sun found her daughter dead, she went into the house and grieved. The people now did not die from the sun's heat, but the world was dark all the time because the sun would not come out.

The people went again to the Little Men, who told them: "If you want the sun to come out again you must bring back her daughter from Tsusginai, the ghost country."

The Little Men chose seven men to go and gave each a sour-wood rod. The men also were to take a box. "When you reach Tsusginai you will find the ghosts at a dance," the Little Men said. "Stand outside the circle, and when the sun's daughter passes in the dance, strike her with your rods until she falls to the ground. Then you must put her in the box and bring her back to her mother.

"You must be sure not to open the box, even a little way, until you reach home."

The men took the box and the rods and traveled seven days to the west until they reached the ghost country. Many people were there having a dance. The sun's daughter was in the outside circle, and as she swung around to where the seven men were standing, one struck her with his rod. She turned and saw him. As she came around the second time another man touched her with his rod, and then another and another, until at the seventh round she fell out of the ring. The men put her into the box and closed the lid fast. The other ghosts seemed not to notice what had happened.

The men started home carrying the box. In a little while the sun's daughter revived and begged to be let out of the box. But the men did not answer and kept walking.

Again the woman called out, "I am hungry. Give me something to eat." Still the men ignored her. After a while she called for something to drink, begging so pitifully that the men found it difficult to ignore her. But they said nothing and kept moving.

At last, as they were very near home, the sun's daughter called again. "Please raise the lid just a little. I am smothering." The men were afraid she was really drying, so they lifted the lid a little to give her air. But as they did so there was a fluttering sound inside the box, and something flew past them into a near-by thicket. They heard a redbird cry, "Kwish! Kwish! Kwish!" in the bushes.

The men shut down the lid and continued their journey home. But when they got home and opened the box, it was empty.

So we know the redbird is the daughter of the sun. If the men had kept the box closed, as the Little Men had told them to do, they would have brought the sun's daughter home safely. We could bring back our other friends also from the ghost country. But now when they die we can never bring them back.

The sun had been happy when the seven men started to the ghost country, but when they came back without her daughter she grieved. "My daughter, my daughter, " she cried. She wept until her tears made a flood on the earth and the people were afraid the world would be drowned.

They held another council and sent their handsomest young men and women to amuse the sun so that she would stop crying. The young people danced before the sun and sang their best songs. For a long time the sun kept her face covered and paid no attention. At last the drummer suddenly changed the song, and she lifted her face. The sun was so pleased at the sight of the dancers and the sound of the music that she forgot her grief and smiled.

This story came from three storytellers: Swimmer, John Ax, and James Blythe. Ax's Cherokee name was Itagunahi. Born about 1800, he was a very old man when he told his stories to James Mooney; he remembered events of the Creek Indian War (1813-14) and the signing away of the tribe's lands in 1819. Although not a professional medicine man, he was recognized as an authority in tribal customs and was an expert in making rattles, wands, and other ceremonial paraphernalia. Ax especially loved stories about giants, the great Uktena, and the invisible spirit people; but he also enjoyed the humorous animal stories. At almost one hundred years of age he walked without assistance, except for his stick, to a ball game, where "he watched every run with interest."

The Milky Way
SEMINOLE

A long while back the Breath-maker blew his breath toward the sky and made the Milky Way. This white way leads to a city in the west where Big Cypress Seminoles go when they die. The Milky Way shines brightest when showing a departed soul the path that leads to the City in the Sky.

Bad people stay in the ground right where they are buried. Every time someone goes through the woods and steps where a bad person is buried, he feels afraid, even though the grave is covered over with bushes.

Robert F. Greenlee recorded this story in Florida

White Dog's Road

CHOCTAW

Long, long ago a hunter living up in the sky had a bag of meal stolen from him by a white dog.

As the dog ran across the sky, the bag came untied. The meal was scattered in a broad white trail, which from that day has been known as the White Dog's Road (Milky Way).

An aged Choctaw told this to Henry Halbert in 1904.

The Moon Is a Ball

CHEROKEE

The moon is a ball that was thrown up against the sky in a game.

Long, long ago two towns were playing each other in a ball game. One town, which had the better runners, had almost won, when the leader of the other town dropped his stick and picked up the ball with his hands and threw it toward the goal. But the ball hit the sky vault and stuck there.

It was a rule of the game that a player could never touch the ball with his hands. So the moon reminds players not to cheat. When the moon is small and pale, someone has cheated.

The Origin of the Pleiades and the Pine

CHEROKEE

Long ago, when the world was new, seven boys spent all their time down by the council house playing the *gatayusti* game. In this game they rolled a stone wheel along the ground and slid a curved stick after it to strike it.

The boys' mothers scolded them about spending all their time playing, but scolding did no good. So one day the women collected some of the *gatayusti* stones and put them in the dinner pot to boil with the corn.

When the boys came home hungry their mothers dipped out the stones and said, "Since you like the *gatayusti* better than the cornfield, you can have them for dinner."

The boys went angrily off to the council house. "Our mothers are mistreating us. Let's go where we will never trouble them again."

They began to dance, leaping round and round the council house, calling to the spirits to help them.

Their mothers worried that something had happened to their sons and went to look for them. Arriving at the council house, they saw the boys dancing. As they watched, the mothers noticed that the boys' feet were off the ground, and that with every round they rose higher and higher in the air.

The women dashed to get their children, but it was too late. The boys were already higher than the council house roof—all but one, whose mother managed to pull him down with the *gatayusti* pole. But the boy struck the ground so hard that he sank into it and the earth closed over him.

The other six boys circled higher and higher and higher until they reached the sky. We see them there now as the Pleiades,

which the Cherokees still call Anitsutsa (the Boys).

The mother whose boy had sunk into the ground visited the spot every morning and evening to cry. She wept so much that the earth became damp with her tears.

At last a little green shoot sprouted on the spot. It grew until it became the tall tree we now call the pine.

The pine, then, shares the same origin as the stars and holds in itself the same bright light.

The Snake That Chased the Moon

NATCHEZ

One night, a little after dark, a boy and his grandmother went to the cow lot to turn the cows out. They heard a noise—wid-zid-zid-zid-ziti— and, looking up at the sky, they saw a snake chasing the moon. They were so frightened that they ran back to the house without letting the cows out.

From the doorway they watched the snake chase the moon across the sky to the western horizon and stop. The snake had markings like a diamondback rattler's, and something on its tail like rattles. As the snake moved its head back and forth, the boy saw something green like a snake's tongue.

After awhile the snake became still, and the boy went back into the house to sleep. Every few minutes, however, the grandmother went to the door to look at the snake. Then she dozed off. Finally, she looked once more and could see nothing of the snake. The moon had gone back to the east to the place where it had started.

Stars Visit the Earth

CHEROKEE

 There are different opinions about the stars. Some say they are balls of light. Others say they are human. but most people say they are living creatures covered with luminous feathers or fur.

One night a hunting party camping in the mountains noticed two lights like large stars moving along the top of a distant ridge. In amazement the hunters watched until the lights disappeared on the other side. Again the next night, and the next, they saw lights moving along the ridge. They decided to investigate.

The next morning they started out. On the ridge they found two strange creatures. Each creature was the size of a man, with a round body from which a small head stuck out like a turtle's. The creatures' bodies were covered with downy feathers. As the breeze played on the feathers, showers of sparks flew out.

The hunters led the strange creatures back to camp, where they stayed for several days. At night, the hunters noticed, they grew bright and shone like great stars. By day they were only balls of down feathers, except when the wind stirred and made the sparks fly.

The creatures kept very quiet, and no one thought they would try to escape. But on the seventh night they suddenly rose from the ground like balls of fire and were soon above the tops of the trees.

Higher and higher they rose, while the hunters watched, until at last they were only two bright points of light in the dark sky. Then the hunters knew that they were stars.

5

Animals and Tricksters

Indians lived closes to nature, and animals were a part of their daily life. The forests and fields and streams where they lived abounded with animals: bears, deer, wolves, panthers, wildcats, possums, raccoons, turkeys, woodpeckers, turtles, snakes, frogs. So we should not be surprised at the role of animals in the Indians' stories.

The animals in most of these stories are, in Indian belief, the original creatures of ancient times who lived as equals with human beings. They spoke the same language and even had chiefs and council meetings. The animals of today, the Indians say, are not descendants of the original animals; they are smaller and less intelligent imitations of those long-ago mythical creatures.

The rabbit is the trickster hero of the southern Indians. In western Indian stories the coyote plays that role. In European stories the troublemaker is Reynard the Fox.

The rabbit in these stories possesses supernatural powers; he is a hero because he can do what no one else can, such as stealing the first fire and bringing it over the ocean (p. 44). He is a free spirit who defies authority and has no respect for taboos. He clowns, he cheats, he lies, he changes his identity whenever he pleases. We admire the rabbit's cleverness although sometimes he becomes the victim of his own pranks. No matter what the rabbit is up to, we know we will be amused and that we will learn a lot about human nature.

The Animals' Ball Game
CHEROKEE

Once the animals challenged the birds to a ball game, and the birds accepted. The leaders made the arrangements and fixed the day, and when the time came, the animals met on a smooth, grassy field near the river and the birds in the treetops by the ridge.

The captain of the animals was the bear. "I am so big and strong," the bear boasted, "I can pull down anyone that gets in my way."

All along the road to the ball game, the bear tossed up huge

The favorite sport of the southern Indians was simply called "the ball game." It was played with a small deerskin ball and long sticks. Sometimes called stickball, it was known also as the Little Brother of War, because opposing groups sometimes vented their anger by "fighting it out" on the playing field. (Indians to the north played a variation called lacrosse.) Stickball is still played by some southern Indians.

James Mooney heard this story, or part of it, from several Cherokee storytellers: John Ax, Swimmer, Suyet, and Awanita of the eastern band in North Carolina and James Wafford in the western Indian Territory.

logs to show his great strength.

The turtle, not the little one we have today but the great original turtle, was with the animals too. "My shell is so hard," he said, "the heaviest blows cannot hurt me." He kept rising to a standing position on his back legs and dropping with a great thud to the ground. "This is the way I will crush any bird that tries to take the ball from me," he said.

"Give me the ball," the deer bragged. "I can outrun any other animal."

Altogether it was a fine company.

The birds had the eagle for their captain. They also had the hawk and the great Tlanuwa, all swift and strong of flight. But they were still a little afraid of the animals.

They were all pruning their feathers up in the trees and waiting for the captain to give the word, when here came two little things hardly larger than field mice, climbing up the tree in which the bird captain perched. At last they reached the top; and, creeping along the limb to where the eagle captain sat, they said, "We want to join in the game."

The eagle, seeing they had four feet, said, "Why don't you play with the animals, where you belong?"

"We tried," they replied, "but the animals laughed at us because we are so small. They drove us away."

The eagle captain felt sorry for the little creatures. "But how can you join us if you have no wings?" he asked. He decided to consult the other birds about this. At last it was decided to make some wings for the little fellows.

"What about the drumhead, made of groundhog skin," someone suggested. "We could cut off a corner and make wings of it."

So they took two pieces of leather from the drumhead and cut them into wing shapes, and stretched them with cane splints and fastened them on to the forelegs of one of the small animals. In this way Tlameha, the bat, came to be.

"Now catch the ball," the birds said to Tlameha, tossing it in the air.

Tlameha circled and dived about, keeping the ball always in the air. The birds saw that the bat would be one of their best players.

"What can we do to fix the other little animal?" the birds wondered. "We have used all our leather to make the bat's wings."

"Perhaps we might do it by stretching his skin," the hawk suggested.

So two large birds took hold of the little animal from opposite sides with their strong bills, and by pulling at his fur for several minutes they managed to stretch the skin on each side between the fore and hind feet, until they had Tewa, the flying squirrel.

"Let us see if he can fly," said the eagle captain. He threw up the ball, and the flying squirrel sprang off the tree limb after it, caught it in his teeth, and carried it through the air to another tree across the field.

When everyone was ready, the signal was given and the ball game began. Almost at the first toss the flying squirrel caught the ball and carried it up a tree. From the tree he threw the ball to the birds, who kept it in the air for some time before it dropped.

The bear rushed to get the ball, but the martin darted after it and threw it to the bat, who was flying near the ground. By his dodging and doubling, the bat kept the ball out of the way of even the deer.

Finally the bat threw the ball between the posts and won the game for the birds.

The bear and the turtle, who had boasted of what they could do, never got a chance to touch the ball.

For saving the ball when it dropped, the martin was presented a gourd in which to build his nest, and he still has it.

Alligator Gets a Broken Nose

SEMINOLE

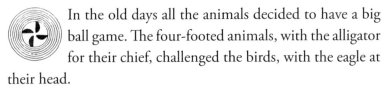 In the old days all the animals decided to have a big ball game. The four-footed animals, with the alligator for their chief, challenged the birds, with the eagle at their head.

Sides were chosen, the poles put up, and the ground measured off. The medicine men put a spell on the balls. On the day of the game, the animals, all painted and dressed up, ran around their poles, while the birds flew and screamed around their poles.

At last the ball was tossed into the air and the game began. The alligator caught the ball in his teeth and ran toward the poles. The birds vainly tried to snatch the ball from him.

The eagle, however, soared high in the air until he was almost out of sight. Then, like an arrow, he swooped to earth and struck the alligator on the nose.

The alligator's wife had been running down the field shouting, "Look at the little striped alligator's daddy! Just look at him!" while the animals shouted in triumph.

But when the eagle hit the alligator, everything changed. The alligator's teeth opened on the ball, and the turkey poked his head in among the teeth, pulled the ball out, and ran to the birds' poles and threw the ball between them.

The birds won the game, and ever since that time the alligator has had a sunken place on his noise where the eagle broke it.

Told by a Seminole named Fixco to William O. Tuggle.

Tricking the Tie-Snakes

HITCHITI

Rabbit said to a tie-snake, "I am strong. I think I am stronger than you."

But the tie-snake replied, "You cannot beat me in a contest of strength."

"Well then, let's set a day when we will test our strength, to see which is the stronger."

The tie-snake said, "All right."

Rabbit went on his way and met another tie-snake. "I am strong," said Rabbit to the second tie-snake.

"Well then, we must set a day on which to have a contest to see which is the stronger."

The tie-snake agreed, and Rabbit proposed the same day as that on which he was to meet the other snake.

On the appointed day Rabbit carried a long grapevine to the first tie-snake. "Catch the end of this," he instructed, "and I will stay in the bend of the creek holding the other end."

He left the first tie-snake and, holding the other end of the grapevine, went to the other tie-snake. "Hold this vine and stay at this end," he said.

To both snakes he said, "When I whoop, I

am ready; that is the signal to pull as hard as you can." Then he went to a spot halfway between the two tie-snakes, sat down, and whooped.

At the sound of the whoop, both tie-snakes pulled with all their strength, trying to drag off Rabbit, who they believed was at the other end of the vine. Both tie-snakes could hear Rabbit shouting, "You can't drag me away." But they were pulling against each other.

Finally Rabbit shouted, "That's enough." He ran to one of the tie-snakes and said, "Am I not strong?"

"You are very strong," the tie-snake said.

Then Rabbit ran to the second tie-snake and said, "Am I not strong?" And the second tie-snake answered, "I didn't know you were that strong. Now I have found out."

Not long after the contest the two tie-snakes met. During the conversation one said, "Rabbit and I tried our strength against each other."

The other said, "He also contested with me."

They they both realized what Rabbit had done to them. Angrily they discussed what they could do to pay him back.

"We won't let him have any water," one said, "so he will die of thirst."

Rabbit did become thirsty, but in going about he met a fawn. "Lend me your coat," he said. The fawn gave him his coat, and Rabbit put it on and went down to the creek.

He was in the water when one of the tie-snakes came by. "I understand there is trouble about getting water," said Rabbit, "but I am very thirsty."

"Only Rabbit is forbidden to drink," the tie-snake said, not recognizing Rabbit in his fawn disguise. "Drink all you want."

Later the tie-snakes found that Rabbit had tricked them again. "We can't do anything with him," they said. "Let him drink the water."

Why Possum's Tail Is Bare

CHEROKEE

Possum used to have a long, bushy tail and was so proud of it that he combed it out every morning and sang about it. Rabbit, who had had no tail since Bear pulled it out, was jealous and made up his mind to play a trick on Possum.

A great council and a dance were planned at which all the animals would be present. It was Rabbit's business to spread the news, so at Possum's place he stopped to ask if he intended to be there.

Possum said he would come if he could have a special seat, "because I have such a handsome tail that I ought to sit where everyone can see me."

Rabbit promised to attend to it and also to send someone to comb and dress Possum's tail for the dance. So Possum agreed to come.

Rabbit went to Cricket, who is such an expert haircutter that the Indians call him the barber, and told him to go next morning and dress Possum's tail for the dance that night. He told Cricket just what to do and went on about some other mischief.

In the morning Cricket went to Possum's house. "I've come to get you ready for the dance." So Possum stretched out and shut his eyes while Cricket combed out his tail and wrapped a red string around it to keep it smooth until night.

But all this time, as he wound the string around, Cricket was clipping off the hair close to the roots, and Possum never knew it.

That night Possum arrived at the dance and found the best seat ready for him, just as Rabbit had promised. When his turn came in the dance he loosened the string from his tail and stepped to the middle of the dance floor. The drummers began to drum and Possum began to sing, "See my beautiful tail."

Everybody shouted, and he danced again around the circle singing, "See what a fine color it has."

Everyone shouted again, and he danced around another time singing, "See how it sweeps the floor."

The animals shouted louder than ever, and Possum was delighted. He danced around again and sang, "See how fine the fur is."

Then everyone laughed so long that Possum wondered if something was wrong. He looked around at everyone and saw that they were laughing at him.

He looked down at his tail. There was no hair on it! It was as bare as a lizard's tail.

Possum was so astonished and ashamed that he rolled over on the floor and grinned, as Possum does to this day when he is taken by surprise.

Tar Wolf and Rabbit
CHEROKEE

Once there was such a long spell of dry weather that the water in the creeks dried up, and the animals held a council to see what to do about it. They decided to dig a well. All agreed to help except Rabbit, who said, "I don't need to dig for water. The dew on the grass is enough for me."

The others did not like Rabbit's attitude, but they set to work digging the well.

They noticed as the days went by that Rabbit kept sleek and lively, although the weather was still dry and the water was getting low in the well. They said, "That tricky Rabbit steals our water at night."

So they made a tar wolf out of pine gum and tar and set it up by the well to scare the thief.

That night Rabbit came, as he had been coming every night, to drink enough to last him all the next day. He saw the queer black thing by the well and said, "Who's there?"

Rabbit came nearer, but the tar wolf did not move. Rabbit grew braver and said, "Get out of my way or I'll hit you." Still the wolf did not move. Rabbit hit him with his paw. The gum held his foot and he could not shake it free.

"Let me go or I'll kick you," he said angrily to the tar wolf. Rabbit struck again with his hind foot, so hard that his foot caught solidly in the gum and he could not move. There he stuck until the animals came for water in the morning.

When they found who the thief was, they made great sport over him for awhile and then got ready to kill him. But as soon as they loosed Rabbit from the tar wolf, he ran away and could not be caught.

The similarity of this story to the Uncle Remus "Wonderful Tar Baby" story by Joel Chandler Harris is obvious. Harris was a friend of William Tuggle and had read Tuggle's collection of Creek myths in manuscript form before he wrote the Uncle Remus story. The tar-baby motif actually is found in many cultures.

"Tar Wolf" was told by James Wafford, a Cherokee living in Indian Territory in the west. Wafford, whose Cherokee name meant "Worn-out Blanket," was born in Georgia, in the old Cherokee Nation, in 1806. His mother was a cousin of Sequoyah.

Master-of-Breath Tests Rabbit

CREEK

 Rabbit went to the Master-of-Breath and asked him for wisdom. "I haven't much sense and want you to give me more," he said.

The Master-of-Breath gave Rabbit a sack. "Fill it with small red ants," he said, "and I will teach you sense." The Master felt that if Rabbit had no sense he couldn't get one ant into the sack.

Rabbit went to the ant hill and said to the ants, "The Master says you cannot fill this sack, but I say you can. What do you think?"

The ants answered, "We will fill the sack." As they were eager to show that they could do so, they all went in. As soon

as they were all in, Rabbit tied up the sack. He carried it back to the Master.

"Here is the sack. Now give me some knowledge."

The Master said, "There is a big rattlesnake over yonder. If you bring him to me, I will give you some knowledge." He thought, *If Rabbit is really ignorant he won't know what to do.*

Rabbit cut a stick and went to find the snake. When he had found him, he said, "The Master says you are not as long as this stick. But I say you are longer."

"Yes, I think I am longer," said the rattlesnake. "Measure me." Rabbit measured him by laying the stick beside him with the sharp point toward the snake's head; as the snake stretched out, Rabbit ran the point into his head and killed him. He carried the rattlesnake to the master on the end of the stick.

Next the Master said, "There is an alligator over yonder in the lake. Bring him to me and I will give you knowledge."

Rabbit went to the lake and called out, "*Halpata hadjo, halpata hadjo.*" This is a respectful term the Creeks used for the alligator.

The alligator poked his head out of the water. "What's the matter?" he said.

"An ox has been killed for the Master and they want you to come and get timbers for a scaffold on which to roast it."

The alligator came out of the water and followed Rabbit. Before they had gone far Rabbit turned around and hit him with a club. The alligator started for the lake. Rabbit chased him, beating him with the club, but the alligator got safely back in the water.

Rabbit now went off for awhile to lie in the sunshine and think. He decided to change his appearance so the alligator would not recognize him. After he had done this, he called to the alligator, "*Halpata hadjo, halpata hadjo.*" And again the alligator stuck his head out of the water and asked, "What's the matter?"

Rabbit called out, "Rabbit was sent here sometime ago and nobody knows what happened to him, so they sent me to ask if you know anything about him."

The alligator said that someone had indeed come and had beaten him.

"They thought he might have done something like that," said Rabbit, "for he is a mean, devilish kind of person. When he didn't come back, they sent me to find out what happened."

The alligator came out of the water and walked along with Rabbit. Rabbit said, "That Rabbit is very bad; they should not have sent him. He has no sense. Did he beat you badly?"

"He beat me hard," said the alligator, "but he did not hit a dangerous place."

"If he had hit you in a dangerous spot would you have lived?"

"No. It would certainly have killed me."

"Where would one have to hit to hurt you?"

"If someone hit me across the hips it would finish me," said the alligator.

Having learned what he wanted to know, Rabbit hit the alligator across the hips and watched him fall dead. Then he picked him up and took him to the Master.

When the Master saw Rabbit he said, "You have more sense than I could give you. But come to me."

Rabbit went up to the Master, who pulled his ears up and down and then stretched both until they stood straight up. Then the Master slapped first one cheek and then the other until both cheeks were flat.

And that is how Rabbit looks to this day.

How Deer Tricked Rabbit

CHEROKEE

In the beginning Deer had no horns; his head was smooth like a doe's. He was a great runner, and Rabbit was a great jumper. The animals were curious to know which could run faster.

"Let's have a race," they said. "We will start Deer and Rabbit off together on one side of the thicket. They will have to go through the thicket, turn around, and come back. The first one back will win the prize, a large pair of antlers."

On the day of the race all the animals were there. The antlers had been put on the ground at the edge of the thicket to mark the starting point. While everyone was admiring the horns, Rabbit said, "I don't know this part of the country. I want to take a look through the bushes where I am to run." Everyone thought that was all right, so Rabbit went into the thicket. But when several minutes went by and Rabbit did not return, the animals suspected he must be up to something.

They sent a messenger to look for him. In the middle of the thicket the messenger found Rabbit gnawing down the bushes and pulling them away to clear a path for himself. The messenger turned around quietly so Rabbit could not hear him and came back to the animals.

"Rabbit is clearing a path for himself so he can win the race," he said.

Just then Rabbit appeared, "I have looked over the thicket," he announced. "I am ready to go."

"You are a cheat," the animals said.

"We know you have cleared a path for yourself." Rabbit denied it. "You are not only a cheat. You are a liar also."

So the animals gave the prize horns to Deer, who has worn them ever since.

To Rabbit the animals said, "You are so fond of cutting down bushes, you can do that for a living from now on."

Rabbit was angry because Deer had won the horns, and he resolved to get even. One day he stretched a grapevine across the trail and gnawed it nearly in two in the middle. Then he went back, took a good run, and jumped up at the vine. He kept on running and jumping at the vine until Deer came along.

"What are you doing?" said Deer.

"Don't you see?" said Rabbit. "I'm so strong that I can bite through that grapevine at one jump."

Deer could hardly believe this, and wanted to see it done. So Rabbit ran back, made a tremendous spring, and bit through the vine where he had already gnawed it.

"Well," said Deer, "if you can do that, so can I."

So Rabbit cut a fresh grapevine and stretched it across the trail. Deer ran back as he had seen Rabbit do, leaped, and struck the grapevine, but it only flew back and threw him over on his head. He tried again and again, until he was bruised and bleeding.

At last Rabbit said, "Let me see your teeth." Deer showed him his teeth, which were long like a wolf's but not very sharp.

"No wonder you can't do it," said Rabbit. "Your teeth are too blunt to bite anything. Let me sharpen them for you. My teeth are so sharp that I can cut through a stick just like a knife."

Rabbit got a hard stone with rough edges and filed and filed away at Deer's teeth until they were worn down almost to the gums.

"That hurts," said Deer. But Rabbit assured him it was supposed to hurt, so Deer kept quiet.

"Now try it," said Rabbit. So Deer tried again, but this time he could not bite the grapevine at all.

"Now you've paid for your horns," laughed Rabbit as he jumped away through the bushes. Ever since then Deer's teeth are so blunt that he cannot chew anything but grass and leaves.

Deer was angry at Rabbit for filing his teeth, and he determined to get revenge. He pretended to be friendly with Rabbit until he could catch him off his guard.

One day as they were walking along talking, Deer challenged Rabbit to a jump. Rabbit is a great jumper, as everyone knows, so he agreed at once.

There was a small stream beside the path, and Deer said, "Let's see if you can jump across this stream. We'll go back a piece, and when I say 'Ku!' we'll both run and jump."

They backed up to get a good start. When Deer said "Ku!" they ran for the stream. Rabbit made one jump and landed on the other side.

But Deer stopped on the bank and did not jump. When Rabbit looked back, Deer had changed the stream so that it was a wide river.

Rabbit was never able to get back again and is still on the other side.

How the Turkey Got His Wattle

SEMINOLE

The turkey was once the king of the birds and flew high like an eagle. He would swoop down on a council ground and carry a person away.

"We must plan a way to catch him," said the people.

Four men rolled four big balls on the ball ground to catch the turkey's attention as he circled high in the air above them. Four other men, fast runners, watched the turkey; as soon as he swooped down, their task was to seize him.

But when the turkey flew down, the four swift warriors saw

the scalp of his last victim hanging around his neck and they were afraid to touch him. An old dog, instead, grasped the turkey by the leg, allowing the people to kill him.

Ever since that time, turkeys have been afraid of people, but even more fearful of dogs. And the turkey gobbler still wears the scaly lock at his breast as a trophy of his former valor.

Although a Seminole story, this was told by a Creek to William O. Tuggle.

How Day and Night Came

CREEK

The animals held a meeting, and the bear presided. The question was: how shall day and night be divided? Some wanted it always to be daytime; others wanted it always to be night.

After much talk, the chipmunk said: "I see that the raccoon has rings on his tail divided equally, first a dark color and then a light color. I think day and night should be divided like the rings on the raccoon's tail."

The animals were surprised at the wisdom of the chipmunk. They adopted his plan and divided day and night like the rings on the raccoon's tail, one succeeding the other in regular order.

The bear was so envious of the chipmunk's wisdom and of the attention given that small creature, that he attacked him. He scratched the chipmunk's back so deeply that even today chipmunks have stripes on their backs.

How Snakes Got Their Poison

CHOCTAW

Pisatuntema, a Louisiana Choctaw, told this story to David I. Bushnell, Jr., in 1910. She had heard it from her father. While telling the story, Pisatuntema was interrupted by other Choctaws who added details, but at no point did they differ on essential parts of the story.

Long ago a vine grew in shallow water along the edge of bayous. The vine was very poisonous. Often when Choctaws bathed or swam in the bayous they came in contact with the vine and became so badly poisoned they would die.

But the vine liked the Choctaws and did not want to cause them trouble and pain. He would poison people without being able to let them know he was beneath the water. So he decided to rid himself of the poison.

The vine called together the chiefs of the snakes, bees, wasps, and other similar creatures. "I want to give you my poison," he said. Up to that time no snake, bee, or wasp had the power it now possesses to sting.

The snakes and bees and wasps, after much talk, agreed to share the poison. The rattlesnake, first to speak, said, "I shall take the poison, but before I strike or poison a person I shall warn him by the noise of my tail—*Intesha*! Then if he does not heed me I shall strike."

The water moccasin spoke next: "I also am willing to take some of your poison. But I shall never poison a person unless he steps on me."

The small ground rattler was the last of the snakes to speak. "Yes, I will gladly take your poison, and I will jump at a person whenever I have a chance." And so the ground rattler has done ever since.

Why Snakes Can Bite

SEMINOLE

Long ago the rattlesnake had no teeth or fangs and was completely harmless.

One day a warrior found a mother rattlesnake with a nest of babies. He killed the babies, but the mother was able to escape.

For three days the mother rattlesnake cried for her babies. At the end of three days, she went to the chief.

"One of your warriors has killed my babies," she said. "I had no weapon to stop him."

"Open your mouth," the chief said.

He made some teeth and fitted them into the rattlesnake's mouth.

"Next time a man comes," he said, "you can bite him."

Since that time, no Seminole will kill a rattlesnake, believing the snake will not bite if left undisturbed.

Robert F. Greenlee recorded this story in Florida in 1939.

How the Bear Lost His Tail

CHOCTAW

Henry S. Halbert heard this story from a Choctaw in Mississippi.

A long time ago the bear had a long tail. He also had a strong odor.

The strong odor was a problem for the bears because hunters were often able to find the bears when the wind blew their scent toward them.

So a bear went to the wind to complain. "You are carrying our scent to the hunters. And we are being killed so fast that soon there will be none of us left."

"All right," the wind agreed, "I will take away the bears' scent. But only on one condition: you must consent to lose your tails."

The bears agreed to this. So the wind cut off their tails.

From that time the bears have no odor, and hunters cannot find them as easily as they did in ancient times.

Rooster and Fox

CATAWBA

The rooster was feeding under a tree when a fox came along. The rooster flew up in the tree to escape.

"Come on down," said the fox. "Don't be scared of me; I won't hurt you. Don't you know peace has been declared between the birds and the animals?"

"No," said the rooster, "I didn't know of it."

"Well, it has. The news has gone around and everybody else has heard of it. So come on down."

From up in the tree, the rooster could see a pack of dogs coming, following the fox's trail. He said, "Well, if that's true, I'll be down directly. I see some dogs coming over the hill to join us."

Before he could finish talking, the fox ran away.

This Aesop-like story was told by Chief Sam Blue some fifty years ago to F.G. Speck and L.G. Carr. The Catawbas, a Siouan-speaking tribe, lived mainly in South Carolina, where they preserved their identity longer than any other tribe of that area. Today about 1,500 Catawbas live on a reservation at Rock Hill. They are noted for their coiled pottery.

A Race Between the Hummingbird and the Crane

CHOCTAW

 A long time ago the hummingbird was a large bird. One day he was perched in a tree near a pond where the crane came to catch fish.

The hummingbird looked at the crane and said, "You are a very big bird, but you cannot fly fast. As for me, I can beat all the birds in flying."

The crane replied angrily, "I bet I can beat you flying to the end of the world and back."

The hummingbird took up the bet. The bargain was that the bird who won could do what he pleased to the loser.

The race began. The hummingbird flew like an arrow shot from a bow, and he soon left the crane far behind.

When night came, the hummingbird stopped to sleep in a cedar tree. The crane had to fly all night to catch up with the

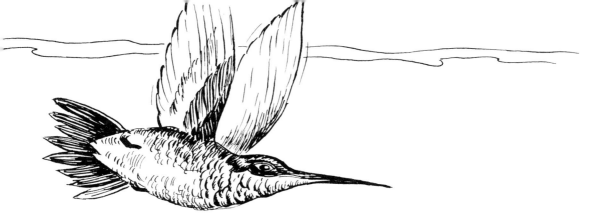

hummingbird. It was daylight when he reached the cedar tree where the hummingbird was sleeping. The hummingbird waked up and again flew far ahead of the crane.

Day after day the two birds flew. The hummingbird flew only in the daytime, and the crane flew both day and night. Day and night were all the same to him.

On the sixth morning, a little after sunrise, the crane reached the end of the world. He waited for the hummingbird. But it was nearly midday before the hummingbird arrived. They both ate, then rested.

The next morning the two birds started back, the hummingbird flying only in the daytime, the crane both day and night.

The crane got back to the pond a little while before the hummingbird and won the bet. The crane took a sharp flint and cut the hummingbird down into a very small bird, not much bigger than a butterfly.

This is how the hummingbird became the smallest bird.

Variations of this Choctaw story heard and recorded by Henry Halbert were told by other southern tribes (as is true of many stories in this book). The Cherokee story is much like this one, except the two birds race to win a pretty woman. In a Creek story, the rivals agree to fly from a spot on a stream to the spring at its head; the hummingbird follows the windings of the stream, but the crane takes a direct route above the trees and wins the race

The Hitchitis had a similar story called "Heron and Hummingbird." Since the heron is often mistaken for the crane, it is likely that the bird in these stories is a great blue heron.

How the Turtle Got a Checked Shell

CREEK

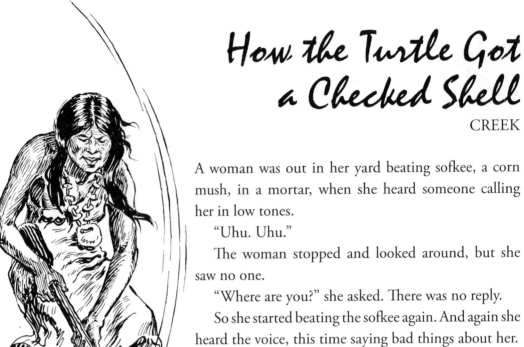

A woman was out in her yard beating sofkee, a corn mush, in a mortar, when she heard someone calling her in low tones.

"Uhu. Uhu."

The woman stopped and looked around, but she saw no one.

"Where are you?" she asked. There was no reply.

So she started beating the sofkee again. And again she heard the voice, this time saying bad things about her.

This made her angry. "I will find you," she said. She searched all around the yard but found nothing. So she came back to her work and was beating the sofkee when she heard, "Uhu, uhu," coming from under the wooden mortar.

She lifted the mortar, and there was a turtle. "How dare you talk to me like that!" She took the pestle and beat the turtle on the back until his shell was broken into little pieces.

"That will teach you a lesson," she said, walking away.

When she was gone, the turtle began to sing in a faint voice:

"Chartee-lee-lee . . . I come together.

Chartee-lee-lee . . . I come together.

Chartee-lee-lee . . . I come together."

The pieces on his broken shell came together as the turtle sang. But his back always looks scarred, and turtles ever since have had checked backs.

Told to William O. Tuggle by a Creek.

How Possums Are Born

CREEK

 When the great flood came, all the animals were put in the big boat except for a pair of possums. The male possum drowned, but the female climbed up on the side of the boat and held on, her tail dragging in the water. When the waters went down, all the hair on her tail had washed off.

All the male possums had drowned, so the female went off alone and coiled herself up as if dead. Her nose was near her side. After she had breathed a long time in this position, little possums appeared in her pouch. In this way possums have been born ever since.

Recorded by William O. Tuggle.

The Ground-Watcher

CHITIMACHA

 When the great deluge came, the people baked a huge earthen pot. In the pot, two people saved themselves, floating on the waters.

With them went two rattlesnakes, who were thought to be the friends of man. In ancient times, the people believed, each house was protected by a rattlesnake, which entered it whenever its owner went away and left when he came back.

During the flood the redheaded woodpecker hooked his claws

into the sky and hung there. The water rose so high that it partly covered his tail; sediment deposited on it by the waters marked it off sharply from the rest of the body, giving the woodpecker the appearance he has today.

After the waters had subsided a little, the woodpecker was sent to find land, but after a long search he came back with no good news.

Then the dove was sent; he returned with a grain of sand. This grain of sand was placed on the sea's surface and made to stretch out in order to form dry land. That is why the dove is called Ground-Watcher; he first saw the ground when the great flood subsided.

This story was recalled by Benjamin Paul, a Chitimacha, and recorded by John R. Swanton. The Chitimachas lived in the lower Mississippi River valley (present-day Louisiana). Some of their descendants live in that area today.

Telling of Legends

CHIEF ELIAS JOHNSON, Tuscarora

. . . It is very difficult for a stranger to rightly understand the morals of [Indian] stories, though it is said by those who know [the Indians] best, that to them the story was always an illustration of some moral or principle.

To strangers they offer all the rites of hospitality, but do not open their hearts. If you ask them they will tell you a story, but it will not be such a story as they tell when alone. They will fear your ridicule and suppress their humor and pathos; so thoroughly have they learned to distrust pale faces, that when they know that he who is present is a friend, they will shrink from admitting him within the secret portals of their heart.

And when you have learned all that language can convey, there are still a thousand images, suggestions and associations recurring to the Indian, which can strike no chord in your heart. The myriad voices of nature are dumb to you, but to them they are full of life and power.

From *Cry of the Thunderbird: The American Indian's Own Story*, Edited and with an Introduction and Commentary by Charles Hamilton. New edition copyright 1972 by the University of Oklahoma Press.

About the Illustrations

The book's illustrations are the artist's interpretations of the fact and fantasy embodied in the stories. They reflect careful attention to detail and authenticity, both in the culture and history of the southern Indians and in the animal and plant life of the southern United States.

The frontispiece is based on an actual prehistoric shell gorget depicting fighting monsters.

At the beginning of each section, the artist has illustrated some of the events and characters identified with stories that follow:

Page 16 (How the World Began): animals in the Upper World, with the earth below held up by cords; a drop of blood from the sun; two figures emerge from the navel of the earth; a buzzard flies over the void; a dog leads migrating people.

Page 42 (Gifts of the Great Spirit): clockwise from top-Rabbit (Eastern cottontail) with flaming sticks of resin in his cap; button snakeroot and redroot. herbal medicines; white-tailed deer; a medicine bag; koonti plant; water spider with tush bowl: corn plant; sacred fire laid with cars of corn; ceremonial pipe; tobacco plant; bear and turkey; (center) smallmouth bass.

Page 70 (Monsters, Heroes, and Spirits): clockwise from top-Tlanuwa. the giant hawk; whirlpool; giant lizard; great turtle; Spear-finger, the stone-fingered witch; Uktena, monster with bat wings, rattlesnake body, and deer antlers; Florida panther; (center) Creek hunter.

Page 106 (Sun, Moon, and Stars): clockwise from top-Wren and Buzzard set the sun in place; star creatures; dancing boys become the Pleiades; a pine tree: dog with meal bag; the moon, wife of the sun; (center) eye and hand symbol of the sun and the supreme being.

Page 122 (Animals and Tricksters): clockwise from top-black

bear; possum; cricket; ruby-throated hummingbird; great blue heron; king snake (tie-snake); turtle; bald eagle; American alligator; turkey; bat; white-tailed deer; (center) Eastern cottontail rabbit.

The circular design introducing stories throughout the book was found on pottery in a mound at Etowah, Georgia. This symbol was of great importance to the southern Indians. The circles represent the universe. The cross inside the circles represents the four directions.

About the Illustrator

Nathan H. Glick, a native of Birmingham, went from high school in Montgomery, Alabama, to four years of art school in New York City where he studied with outstanding teachers such as Eric Pape and George Ennis, At the same time he worked under James L. Clarke at the American Museum of Natural History, studying animal anatomy, Later he returned to Montgomery as art director for the Paragon Press. During this time he illustrated several books on Alabama history by Marie Bankhead Owen, director of the State Department of Archives and History. When Mrs. Owen conceived the idea of bronze doors for the Archives building, Glick was chosen as the designer for the monumental work depicting eight scenes in Alabama history.

In World War II, Glick served as a combat artist for the Ninth Air force, and his work appeared in *Yank*, *Stars and Stripes*, *London Illustrated*, *Life*, and *Parade*. His war work has been exhibited in Cairo, London, and Paris.

After the war, Glick moved back to Birmingham to join *Progressive Farmer Magazine* as associate art editor and illustrator. In 1983, he illustrated *The World of the Southern Indians* by Virginia Pounds Brown and Laurella Owens.

He is currently painting, illustrating, and working on murals.

Bibliography

This is not a complete bibliography of southern Indian myths and legends, and it does not include many of the publications consulted by the compilers of this book. It is a listing, first, of the specific sources from which stories were drawn, and second, of related materials which would be helpful to readers wishing to read further about this subject. Books marked * are especially recommended for young people.

STORY SOURCES

Bushnell, David I., Jr. *The Choctaw of Bayou Lacomb*. Bureau of American Ethnology Bulletin, no. 48. Washington, D.C., 1909.

———. "Myths of the Louisiana Choctaw." *American Anthropologist* 12(1910):526-535.

Gatschet, Albert S. *A Migration Legend of the Creek Indians*, vol. I. Brinton's Library of Aboriginal American Literature, no. IV. New York: AMS Press, 1969.

Greenlee, Robert. F. "Folktales of the Florida Seminole." *Journal of American Folklore* 58(1945):138-144.

Hatfield, Dorothy Blackmon, and Current-Garcia, Eugene. "William Orrie Tuggle and the Creek Indian Folk Tales." *Southern Folklore Quarterly* 25(1961):238-255.

MacCauley, Clay. "Seminole Indians of Florida." *Fifth Annual Report of the Bureau of American Ethnology*. Washington, D.C., 1887, pp. 469-531.

Montgomery, Ala. Alabama Department of Archives and History. Henry Sale Halbert Manuscript Collection

———. Alabama Department of Archives and History. George Stiggins Manuscript Collection.

Mooney, James. "Myths of the Cherokee." *Nineteenth Annual Report of the Bureau of American Ethnology*. Washington, D.C., 1900, pp. 1-576.

Speck, F.G. "Notes on Chickasaw Ethnology and Folklore." *Journal of American Folklore* 20(1907):50-58.

Speck, F.G., and Carr, L.G. "Catawba Folk Tales from Chief Sam Blue." *Journal of American Folklore* 60(1947):79-84.

Sturtevant, William C. "Seminole Myths of the Origin of Races." *Ethnohistory* 10(1963):80-86.

Swanton, John R. *Early History of the Creek Indians and Their Neighbors*. Bureau of American Ethnology Bulletin, no. 13. Washington, D.C., 1922.

———. *Indian Tribes of the Lower Mississippi Valley and Adjacent Coast of Gulf of Mexico*. Bureau of American Ethnology Bulletin, no. 43. Washington, D.C., 1911.

———. *The Indians of the Southeastern United States.* Bureau of American Ethnology Bulletin, no. 137. Washington, D.C., 1946.

———. *Myths and Tales of the Southeastern Indians.* Bureau of American Ethnology Bulletin, no. 88. Washington, D.C., 1929.

———. "Social and Religious Beliefs and Usages of the Chickasaw Indians." *Forty-fourth Annual Report of the Bureau of American Ethnology.* Washington, D.C., 1926-27, pp. 169-273.

———. "Social Organization and Social Usages of the Indians of the Creek Confederacy; Religious Beliefs and Medical Practices of the Creek Indians." *Forty-second Annual Report of the bureau of American Ethnology.* Washington, D.C., 1928, pp.26-672.

———. *Source Material for the Social and Ceremonial Life of the Choctaw Indians.* Bureau of American Ethnology Bulletin, no. 103. Washington, D.C., 1931.

Tuggle, William Orrie. *Shem, Ham, & Japheth: The Papers of W.O. Tuggle.* Edited by Eugene Current-Garcia and Dorothy B. Hatfield, Athens, Ga.: University of Georgia Press, 1973.

Witthoft, John, and Hadlock, Wendell S. "Cherokee-Iroquois Little People." *Journal of American Folklore* 59(1946):413-422.

RECOMMENDED READING

*Bell, Corydon. *John Rattling-Gourd: A Collection of Cherokee Indian Legends.* New York: Macmillan, 1955.

*Brown, Virginia Pounds, and Owens, Laurella. *The World of the Southern Indians.* Birmingham, Ala.: Beechwood Books, 1983.

DeWitt, Dorothy, ed. *The Talking Stone: An Anthology of Native American Tales and Legends.* New York: Greenwillow, 1979.

Erdoes, Richard, and Ortiz, Afonso, eds. *American Indian Myths and Legends.* New York: Pantheon Books, 1984.

Federal Writers' Project of the Works Progress Administration. *Georgia: A Guide to Its Towns and Countryside.* American Guide Series. Athens: University of Georgia Press, 1946.

———. *Mississippi: A Guide to the Magnolia State.* American Guide Series. New York: Viking Press, 1938.

*Gridley, Marion E. *Indian Legends of American Scenes.* Chicago: M.A. Donohue and Co., 1939.

Hudson, Charles. *The Southeastern Indians.* Knoxville, Tenn.: University of Tennessee Press, 1976.

*Jablow, Alta, and Withers, Carl. *The Man in the Moon: Sky Tales from Many Lands.*

New York: Holt, Rinehart and Winston, 1969.

Journal of American Folklore. Washington, D.C., American Folklore Society.

Kilpatrick, Jack Frederick, and Kilpatrick, Anna Gritts. *Friends of Thunder.* Dallas: Southern Methodist University Press, 1964.

*Leach, Maria. *How the People Sang the Mountains Up: How and Why Stories.* New York: Viking, 1967.

*Mariott, Alice, and Rachlin, Carol K. *American Indian Mythology.* New York: T.Y. Crowell, 1968.

*Mooney, James. *Cherokee Animal Tales.* Edited by George F. Scheer. New York: Holiday House, 1968.

National Geographic Society. *The World of the American Indian.* Washington, D.C., 1974.

Peithmann, Irwin M. *The Unconquered Seminole Indians.* St. Petersburg, Fla.: Great Outdoors, 1957.

Radin, Paul. *The Trickster: A Study in American Indian Mythology.* New York: Philosophical Library, 1956.

*Reader's Digest. *America's Fascinating Indian Heritage.* Pleasantville, N.Y.: Reader's Digest, 1978.

Rights, Douglas L. *The American Indian in North Carolina.* Winston-Salem, N.C.: John F. Blair, 1957.

Schoolcraft, Henry Rowe. *Historical and Statistical Information Respecting . . . the Indian Tribes of the United States.* 6 vols. Philadelphia: Lippincott, 1851-1857.

Southern Folklore Quarterly. Gainesville, Fla.: Department of English, University of Florida.

Swanton, John R. *The Indians of the Southeastern United States.* Bureau of American Ethnology Bulletin, no. 137. Washington, D.C.: US Government Printing Office, 1946.

Thompson, Stith. *Tales of the North American Indians.* Cambridge, Mass.: Harvard University Press, 1929.

Walker, Alyce Billings, ed. *Alabama: A Guide to the Deep South.* New rev. ed. Originally compiled by the Federal Writers' Project of the Works Progress Administration. American Guide Series. New York: Hastings House, 1975.

Williams, Samuel C., ed. *Adair's History of the American Indians.* Johnson City, Tenn.: Wautauga Press, 1930.

Williams, Walter L., ed. *Southeastern Indians Since the Removal Era.* Athens: University of Georgia Press, 1979.

*Wood, Marion. *Spirits, Heroes & Hunters from North American Mythology.* New York: Schocken, 1982.

Index